CRONIN'S KEY III

N.R. WALKER

COPYRIGHT

Cover Artist: Sara York
Editor: DJ Mack
Cronin's Key III © 2015 N.R. Walker
Publisher: BlueHeart Press
Second Edition 2017

Warning

Intended for an 18+ audience only. This book contains material that maybe offensive to some and is intended for a mature, adult audience. It contains graphic language, explicit sexual content, and adult situations.

Trademark Acknowledgements:

The author acknowledges the trademarked status and trademark owners of the following wordmarks mentioned in this work of fiction:

- *Merriam Webster*: Merriam Webster, Incorporated
- *Oxford Dictionary:* Oxford University Press
- *Scooby Doo*: Hanna-Barbera
- *Underworld*: Screen Gems
- *All references to Dan Brown, and his work*: Dan Brown, Inc.

DEDICATION

For my readers. Without you, my words would seem impossible.

Cronin's Key III

N.R. Walker

CHAPTER ONE

ALEC SAT BACK in the chair and held in a sigh, feeling every bit the lab rat he'd become. Since he'd changed into a vampire a year ago, he'd been put through test after test, so each and every one of his unending list of talents could be explored and documented.

He'd agreed to this, and he knew it was the right thing to do, but in that very moment, he wished to be doing anything else.

And with talents for making errant thoughts an instant reality—like setting fire to sofas and making Xbox controllers explode in Eiji's hand because he'd somehow won—it wasn't a good frame of mind to be in.

He loved Jodis. He really did. She had become one of his best friends. But she'd also taken it upon herself to document his talents, and he'd just about had enough for one day. If replicating wasn't a talent so frowned upon in the vampire world, he'd make a copy of himself to endure Jodis' tests while he and Cronin hid out in their bedroom. He'd replicated himself a few times, experimentally of course, and found it too taxing on himself anyway.

"Can you do it again?" she asked, notepad and pen in hand.

Alec had found a certain talent he'd dubbed the chameleon, for obvious reasons, because he could make things change color. It was absurd, really, and probably of no better use than a party trick. But he could, if he concentrated, turn a red pen blue or a white shirt black. The talent could only manifest by touch, and it lasted only a few minutes before returning to its original color, but Jodis was rather intrigued.

Alec, on the other hand, had passed bored like it was standing still and was well on his way to irate. "Jodis, I've kinda had enough of this today."

"Last one, I promise."

For Alec, it wasn't so much as reining in a temper anymore, where the most damage done was a cutting remark. Now it was keeping a lid on a few dozen talents that reacted poorly to anger. He only had to get really pissed off and a rage would barrel out of him like nuclear fallout, literally knocking humans and vampires off their feet. Or he could burst eardrums with a furious roar, or maybe he could turn them to stone, or dust. Or maybe, just maybe, he could rip an earthquake through the apartment so he didn't have to do any more of these stupid fucking tests.

"Alec," Eleanor cautioned from the next room.

"I wasn't *actually* going to do that," he replied petulantly. He knew Eleanor, with the gift of foresight, saw possible outcomes of decisions made, and that did nothing to quell his frustration. "Jesus, now my thoughts aren't even my own." Standing up, he snatched the purple notebook off the desk, holding it for half a second and slamming it back down. It was now black, as was every page inside it, and it was smoldering as though it almost caught fire.

Cronin was suddenly in front of him, a hand cupped to his face. "He's had enough," he said to Jodis, and they disappeared.

AS SOON AS Alec's feet hit the soft earth, he took a deep breath of fresh air and reveled in the silence.

His life hadn't exactly been quiet in the last twelve months.

He felt the warmth of Cronin's hand in his, smelled the sweet aromas of heath and moss from both the vampire beside him and the cool air of the long-abandoned battlefield, and Alec exhaled loudly.

Cronin had somehow learned to quiet his mind a little and it gave Alec the silence he so desperately needed. In the last twelve months, Cronin had taken Alec on more *time-outs* than he could count. Knowing when he'd had enough and was reaching his breaking point, Cronin would simply remove Alec from the situation, leaping him somewhere quiet where his mind could have some much needed solitude. But with a gentle squeeze of his hand, Cronin reassured him he was there.

"I'm sorry," Alec said.

"Don't apologize," Cronin said adamantly. "I can't begin to imagine your frustrations."

"Jodis is only trying to help. I behaved badly." He could very well speak words directly into Jodis' mind and tell her privately that he was sorry. But he'd prefer not to invade the thoughts of others, preferring to apologize in person.

"She understands," Cronin said, trying to pacify him.

Alec sighed loudly and allowed the quiet to envelop him. "I love it here," he said eventually.

The field at Dunadd, Scotland, had become a sanctuary for Alec. No voices in his head, no city of millions with flurrying thoughts rushing unbidden through his mind, no politics of vampire councils, no meetings, no one hovering.

Just Cronin.

"It affords you a great privacy," Cronin said. His Scottish accent and formal tone still made Alec smile. "Your talents as a vampire are a burdensome gift."

Alec had learned very early on to block out the voices and thoughts of those around him, but living in such a large city made it a constant effort, and his display of anger at Jodis just minutes ago bothered him. "These talents are a pain in my ass."

Cronin laughed quietly. "Your control over them still astounds us all."

"The control you keep talking about is a talent in itself. It's like casting a net over a thousand different fish." Alec sighed loudly. "I've told you that before."

"I know. Though it amazes me still." Cronin squeezed Alec's hand again and looked out across the field of long grass to the line of trees that fronted the river. "Lie down with me."

Cronin simply lay flat on his back in the middle of the field and when Alec lay down next to him, Cronin snatched up Alec's hand again. And together in the mind-clearing silence, they watched the blanket of stars glide across the sky.

It was a clear autumn night in Scotland, cold and dark. Neither of those things impeded a vampire of course, and Alec would never tire of the simple changes he'd gone through when he became a vampire. It was the complex changes he was beginning to struggle with. The talents he'd been given made him unique: the only vampire ever to have *all* vampire talents, some he was still discovering a year after his change. It was these talents that made his life hectic, his obligations as *the key* to the vampire world that gave him a great responsibility, and as Cronin had said, it was becoming a great burden.

Alec loved that Cronin would leap them to the very field where his human life had ended. The old battlefield in Scotland was also where they'd first made love, where they came to talk, to be by themselves. Like now.

"Thank you for bringing me here," Alec whispered, his anger and frustration from before almost gone. "I feel like I can breathe here."

"Is that not what husbands do?" Cronin asked with a smile. "Save the other from the myriad of madness?"

"Husbands," Alec said, bringing Cronin's knuckles up to his lips and kissing them softly. "Now that is something I'll never tire of. And that place you call a myriad of madness is our home." Since their wedding just six months prior, they'd barely had more than a few hours to themselves. Their apartment was never empty. Alec sighed, still looking at the night sky. "Do you think we could buy this place? That little farmhouse by the hillfort could be our private sanctuary. Just for us."

"Do you wish to?"

Alec snorted quietly. "I was just kidding."

"I will look into it. I rather like that idea myself."

"I wasn't being serious. It was just a random thought. I'm pretty sure husbands don't just go and buy the other one every single thing he thinks of."

Cronin leaned up on his elbow and leaned in so he could kiss Alec softly. "Don't think it would be just for you," he said with a gleam in his eye. "A quiet place where I could have you all to myself is more for my selfish reasons than your romantic whim."

Alec laughed and rolled on top of Cronin. "So when I want a place for us to have some privacy, it's romantic, but when you want some privacy to have your way with me, it's what?"

"Wicked."

Alec grinned down at him. "I happen to like wicked."

"And maybe I could bed you in a place of our own without an audience three rooms away," Cronin added. "And not in some random hotel or muddy field."

Alec brushed his fingers through Cronin's hair. "Random hotels are fun, but going back to the apartment full of people when we're both covered in mud is the most fun of all."

Cronin's eyes crinkled when he smiled. "They were certainly surprised. Though it didn't help that, when asked what on earth we got up to, you showed everyone the mental images."

Alec laughed at the memory. Being able to show other people images in their minds was a talent with some benefits. And just because he could, he ran a reel of images through Cronin's mind, snippets of them making love: flushed skin, hands gripping, thighs open, being joined, heads thrown back in ecstasy. And then, to prove a point, Alec surged out a cloud of what it felt like when they fucked. Empathic transference, allowing Cronin to feel what he was feeling, was one of Alec's favorite talents.

Cronin bucked his hips instantly and growled out, "Alec."

Alec pulled back the images and the lust, leaving Cronin breathless. His black eyes were swimming, swirling with want. He took a hold of Alec's face and brought their mouths together in a searing kiss.

Cronin moved his arms down Alec's back and held him tighter. He rolled his hips up and kissed him deeper until Alec was lost in him.

Then it happened.

Images. Visions flashed through Alec's mind, visions he did not put there. Alec had learned to protect his mind, another of his talents was to shield his own thoughts from others. Yet someone or something had penetrated through.

"Alec, what is it?" Cronin asked.

When Alec looked down at a concerned Cronin, Alec realized he'd zoned out, their make-out session long-forgotten. "We need to leave," Alec said, jumping to his feet. He pulled Cronin up by the hand, and before Cronin could ask why, Alec pulled him close, and they leapt.

CHAPTER TWO

ALEC AND CRONIN'S feet had no sooner hit the floor in the New York City apartment than Alec had called out, "Jodis! Eiji!"

They appeared not a moment later, clearly concerned at the tone of Alec's voice. "What is it?" Eiji asked.

"Eleanor? Did you see that?" Alec asked.

Eleanor was at the table with Kole, and they both stood up. "See what?" She shook her head. "I didn't see anything."

"Someone put a vision in my head," Alec said. "Like they specifically wanted me to see. It was deliberate and aimed at me."

Cronin pulled back so he could look into Alec's eyes. "Tell us. What did you see?"

"I'll show you," Alec said, looking at everyone in the room. Then he recalled the images, and with no more than a wish to do so, he transferred his gift of seeing to the others.

They were used to it now, having Alec transfer a talent to them, and they looked upon the group of strangers in front of them, seeing what Alec had seen.

There were five of them. They looked human on the

outside, but one of Alec's new talents allowed him to see a person's true self, regardless of what outer shell, or skin, they wore.

And shimmering under the surface of their human skins, these *people* were wolf-like, almost goblin-looking creatures that walked on two feet. They had claw-like hands, and humanesque faces with the exception of wolf teeth.

Alec knew where he recognized them from. With pictures flashing through his mind like a film on fast-forward, these creatures looked like the gargoyle statues on castles all over the world. Or similar to the dog-like faces in Aztec and Incan carvings.

There was a collective gasp from everyone in the room as they saw firsthand what Alec had seen.

Kole, Alec's father, being the only human in the room, stated what all the vampires had more than likely already processed. "I can see what they are under their skin. It moves, shimmers, like they're struggling to keep up their human façade."

Alec nodded and pulled the images back into his own mind. He looked at Cronin. "What are they?"

Cronin shook his head slowly, clearly shocked at what he'd just seen. "I don't know."

"They looked familiar in an unfamiliar kind of way," Eiji said. "Which doesn't even make sense."

Everyone nodded slowly though, because Eiji had just summed up what Alec felt earlier, like he had seen them before, but not directly. "I wasn't sure if I'd ever seen them, if something tweaked in my subconscious, or if it was my brain and some unknown mind-talent I couldn't make sense of," Alec added.

"They looked similar to the stone carvings at the

Cholula and Tikal pyramids," Jodis said quietly. "Or at Koh Ker in Cambodia."

Cronin nodded. "Wolves?"

No one answered, remaining wide-eyed and still. Scared, even.

Alec turned to Cronin. "What's a Zoan?"

Cronin thought for a moment, no doubt scanning centuries of memories. "I've not heard of a Zoan. Why do you ask?"

"When I saw them, or when they showed themselves, the word came to me. Whether they told me deliberately or whether the word presented itself to me as part of a talent, I don't know. I can see the truth in people and vampires, what they are underneath, who they present themselves to be. Maybe it's possible the name came to me without their permission." Alec frowned. "It's been a while since things were unknown to me."

"You see nothing else?" Jodis asked. She knew Alec's talents left no stone unturned.

He shook his head. "No."

Eiji's eyebrows furrowed. "Alec, you said, 'When they showed themselves to you.' You think the only reason you saw anything is because they allowed it?"

Alec nodded. "Yes. They wanted me to see them. I had the distinct feeling of them allowing me to see what they showed me."

Cronin started to growl. "I don't like it."

Alec looked at Cronin and pulled a stray blade of grass from the back of his hair that was left over from their all-too-brief romp in the field at Dunadd. He smiled at it. "I didn't like being interrupted either."

"Please, Alec," Cronin said, not amused. "This is no time for jokes."

"Mmm." Jodis obviously agreed with Cronin. "Alec, how do they possess a talent you cannot read or even identify?"

"They're not vampires," Alec stated simply. "They're Zoan." His mind flicked through information like a high-powered computer searching files for a key word. "Zoan comes from the word zoanthropy, right? A word given by doctors in the eighteenth century, meaning a form of madness involving the delusion of being an animal with correspondingly altered behavior. It's often associated with schizophrenia or bipolar disorder." Alec stared at Cronin. "Or clinical lycanthropy."

Then, just as before, the Zoan figures appeared: five dark cloaked figures, this time with their heads bowed. Though now they appeared in the living room, not in Alec's mind.

Alec spun around and waved his hand, casting a protective shield around Cronin and the others. In a nanosecond, he put himself in front of his friends and family and threw out another wave over the intruders, this time a shock of immobility.

The Zoan didn't move, but Alec somehow knew it was their choice to be still, not his.

The leader, the taller one at the point of their arrow formation, lifted its head. It was male, but his human face flickered, barely concealing the grotesque figure underneath.

"What are you doing here?" Alec demanded. He crouched into a defensive position. "How did you get in here?"

"Your mental blockades do not impede us," he said softly.

"What are you?" Alec asked. He felt no immediate

threat from them, like they wanted information not confrontation, but their very uninvited presence was exactly that.

The leader bowed his head. "We have been called many things. We call ourselves Zoan, though given your vampire nature, you may recognize the name *Vukodlak.*"

"What do you want?"

"We came to see if it was true. The human key does indeed exist, though he is not human anymore." The leader looked up and smiled. Alec could feel no malice coming from him, though his smile was a horrifying muzzle full of sharp teeth. "We should thank you."

"For what?"

"For granting us life once more. We were reborn with you." He bowed his head again. "For every birth of light comes the birth of darkness. It is an honor to call you our enemy."

Alec bared his fangs and growled but the leader only laughed. He glanced over Alec's shoulder, and Alec could see into his mind and look through his eyes. Behind Alec stood his friends and family completely silent and still, as though stuck in time.

Alec spun on his heel to face them, to look at a stock-still Cronin. The sound of the Zoan's laughter rang out, and then like a vacuum of sound exploding, time restarted. It literally knocked Alec off his feet.

CHAPTER THREE

"ALEC!" Cronin cried, grabbing him before he hit the floor.

Vampires didn't fall over. They didn't lose their balance, ever. Especially when that vampire had every conceivable talent in the history of vampires: mind reading, foresight, protective shields.... The list was endless. He should be indestructible. Yet Alec looked as though he'd been struck by a great unseen weight that stole the air from his lungs. And Sammy, the cat, arched his back, his fur static, and with a feral hiss, he flew out of the room.

In that split second, Cronin almost took Alec and leapt. His first instinct was to remove Alec from danger, protect and keep him safe. But something told him to stay. "What is it? What happened?" Cronin fussed, putting his hands to Alec's face, searching for anything amiss.

Everyone was clearly alarmed, crowded around him. The room was silent, in shock and waiting.

"Did you not see...?" Alec shook his head. Cronin helped him to his feet, and Alec looked to where the Zoan creatures had stood. "Did you guys not see that?"

"See what?" Cronin asked quietly. It appeared that

Alec looked around the room at the faces staring back at him, waiting for someone to laugh. "Alec, there was nothing to see."

Alec paled. He looked at Eiji and Jodis, then to Kole, and finally back to Cronin. "It wasn't in my head. I swear to you. They were standing right there."

"No, it wasn't in your mind. The cat saw whatever it was you did. Was it the Zoan?" Jodis asked.

Alec took a deep breath and nodded as Eiji disappeared, and Cronin could hear him doing a perimeter check of the apartment. He came back in a second later, his long black hair fanned out with his speed. "We're secure."

Jodis' tone was short and sharp. "Eleanor? Did you see anything?"

Eleanor shook her head. "No. I cannot see them. Only what Alec showed me before. I have no visions of them at all."

"They were right there," Alec said finally, pointing to the space in the living room near the wall of Cronin's antiques. "There were five of them, in a V formation. The leader at the front was the only one who spoke. It was the same people... things, wolves, Zoan, whatever the fuck they are." He looked at Cronin, his eyes pleading, yet wide and wild. "They were right there."

"They spoke to you?" Cronin asked.

Alec nodded.

"What did they say?"

"I can show you," Alec said, quickly looking at everyone. "You'll see I'm not making this up."

Cronin put his hand to Alec's face and spoke low and fervent. "I don't doubt you, Alec. No one here does. You're not going mad. Sammy didn't like their presence either, remember? Show us what you saw so we may share this burden with you."

Alec took one last look at the faces staring back at him, and with no more than a soft breath, he showed them. He'd described this telepathic transference to Cronin once, like extending synapse-like fingers directly from the limbic system. As easy as thinking it himself, he could think it in someone else's head, sharing the memory with whomever he chose, no matter where they were in the world.

And this was a memory. It wasn't a vision. It wasn't a delusion. It was a memory. He saw it, breathed it, lived it.

Just moments ago, there were five of these creatures a few feet from them, and only Alec saw it.

Even through Alec's memory, Cronin could sense time had stood still. He heard them converse, in a space and time that did not exist. It was bizarre and absurd, yet it was the truth.

And as quickly as it appeared in his mind's eye, it was gone. Cronin grabbed Alec by the shirt and pulled him in close. *You're safe, m'cridhe,* he thought, knowing Alec would hear him.

Alec nodded against Cronin's neck before finally pulling back. "You saw it?" he asked collectively.

Everyone nodded, wide-eyed, pale, and speechless.

"What are the Vukodlak?" Kole asked. "I've never heard of them, but he said that's what we'd know them as."

Cronin swallowed hard. He didn't like this. He didn't like this at all. "In centuries past, vukodlak was a name the Greeks used for Vampire. It's also the same name used throughout Eastern Europe for wolf."

"A vampire wolf?" Kole asked. Alec's father looked like he'd aged a year in the last five minutes. "What the hell is a vampire wolf?"

"*Vargulf*. Or *ulfhéðinn*," Jodis murmured. Cronin hadn't seen her look this worried in a very long time. "It's the Norse word for 'one who wears a wolf's skin.'"

"The Japanese would call them *kitsune* or *tanuki*," Eiji said. "Those who can transform to a fox or dog. The Russians call them *bodark*, the Bulgarians call them *vrkolak*. The Mesoamericans called them *Nahual*. There are a dozen names throughout history to depict such a creature."

Alec looked to his father and explained. "There are differences, Dad. But the name you and I would call them is *lycan*."

"Werewolf?" Kole whispered in return.

"Similar, but no. Like Alec said, there are differences between the two," Cronin allowed. "They are lycan."

Alec stared at Cronin. "You told me once there was no such thing."

Cronin shook his head. "Because I did not know."

"If they've had names from different cultures throughout history just like vampires, did anyone not stop and think it's because they might actually exist?" Alec was angry and Cronin couldn't blame him. "Did you not think it a possibility that they would be just as real as vampires?"

"In all my years I've never encountered one or heard of anyone encountering one," Cronin said defensively. "It would be no more feasible for me to assume leprechauns or fairies exist!"

Alec put his hand to the back of Cronin's neck and pulled him against him. "I'm sorry," Alec murmured with a kiss to his head. "I know. I can see that. I didn't mean to raise my voice to you."

Cronin tightened his arms around Alec. They rarely exchanged heated words and it burned as though his heart were on fire in his chest. The feel of Alec's arms around him were a healing balm. "If I had known, if I'd had any idea they existed, or were a threat to you...."

"Well," Eiji interjected. "It's safe to assume they do exist. But the real question is, why did they announce themselves to be Alec's enemy?"

ALEC LOOKED around the busy apartment and suppressed a sigh. There were vampires everywhere, reading what they could, researching what they could. Except for Alec. He sat on the floor with his legs crossed and his eyes closed. To the others he might have looked deep in meditation, but he was actually using the strength of his mind to not only fortify the protective barrier around the apartment but also to put feelers out, reaching into minds all over the world to see if he could taste the word Zoan or lycan anywhere. Even though extending his powers to such levels exhausted him, he had to try. "Someone somewhere must know something," he said, more to himself than to anyone in the room.

Alec had queried calling a council meeting of world elders, but Eiji and Cronin both cautioned against it. "Not until we know more," Eiji said. "If we call a meeting now, it may cause a panic, and that is not something we need to add to our list of worries right now."

"Agreed," Cronin added. "If things get worse, then yes, we make the call. But for now, let us keep our cards close to our chest."

Jodis had given Alec's hand a squeeze. *We'll figure this out, Alec. I promise you.*

Thank you, Alec replied. *And I need to apologize for my*

outburst earlier. I was short tempered and I'm sorry I took it out on you.

She smiled and her blue eyes glistened like ice. *No apologies needed, my dear.* She looked around the living room. *But we should not waste time on this.*

Jacques, the French vampire who had assumed the role of Alec's father's protector, had been a constant since their time in the underground pits in China. As had Eleanor, the seer who had proven herself an important ally. She had also become rather close to Alec's father, which pleased Alec a great deal. But in the last twelve months, they'd been intermittently joined by vampires from all over the world. Things hadn't seemed to stop for a second.

At that very moment, there were six vampires in the apartment and one very human man. Kole was safe; no one would even dare think of harming him. Even with visiting vampires, Alec would hear the thought or even taste their hunger for his blood and either stake them where they stood or leap them to the sunbaked blazing Sahara desert. Either way, wanting to harm Kole would be their last living thought.

They needed an array of reference books for their research, more than what they'd already accrued. Alec could transfer anything, an object or person, to wherever he wanted them leapt. So, with a mental scan, he now searched libraries and the oldest books for words pertaining to Zoan, lycan, or shape-shifter and simply plucked the book from its shelf, making it appear on the table in the apartment.

Alec opened his eyes in time to see Jodis smile brilliantly as the books appeared. And with a small nod at Alec and a mental *thanks,* she picked up the first and started reading.

Cronin, with a stack of books in his arms, sat next to Alec.

Alec, are you well? Cronin thought the question, knowing Alec would hear.

Alec nodded and sent his reply to Cronin's mind. *I am. A little drained but otherwise fine.*

Have you found anything?

No. And I don't think strengthening the shield around us is of any use at all. They waltzed into my mind like they owned it, and I'd already put blocks on all external forces.

It was true. Alec learned very early on that a wall around his own mind would safeguard his sanity. He blocked out the voices, the sounds, the feelings, the powers of those around him, only letting in what he wanted.

I also tried to immobilize the Zoan when they first appeared, but it had no effect. It seems my powers are useless against them. I can read them, a little, or maybe they only show me what they want me to see. Maybe they hold that power over me as well.

Cronin sighed. *When you were enduring their encounter, it was as though no time passed for us. Not even a blink of an eye. Then seeing what you showed us, the meeting lasted for half a minute. It was as though—*

Alec finished Cronin's thought. *—as though time stood still.*

Yes.

Like I was moving, living through it while you were stuck on a moment. Frozen in time. And when time started again, it floored me. Literally.

Alec felt Cronin tense beside him. *We will find out their intentions, Alec. And we will stop them.*

Alec opened his eyes then, looked at Cronin, and gave

him a sad smile. *How? If I have an untapped well of power but am helpless against them, how will we beat them?*

Like we always do. Together.

Alec turned his head a little and smiled. "Jacques," he whispered with a nod to the door.

Then Jacques walked into the living room, holding the whiteboard they'd used to map and plan their battles with first the Egyptian gods and then the Terracotta Army. He grinned as he placed it upright on the table. "Just like old times, yes?"

Alec rose fluidly to his feet and put his hand on Jacques' arm with a smile. "And I thought I'd left my days on the force behind me."

"I thought it would help you," Jacques offered apologetically.

"It does. More than you know," Alec said. He picked up the whiteboard marker and removed the cap and looked around the room. Now, he could read the minds of everyone in the room easily enough, but to form a team and to encourage free-thinking and group discussions, he said, "So, tell me what we know so far, from the beginning."

Jodis answered first. "Well, as you said before, according to Westernized medicine, Zoanthropy is the delusion where one believes he or she is an animal and then acts like one."

Eleanor added, "And we know throughout history, human medical diagnoses are quite often linked to some truth in the... paranormal."

"These Zoan resemble a wolf. We have no records of them in our vampire histories," Jacques said, "though human histories have noted folklores of wolf-like men since the beginning of recordable history. There has to be some truth to that."

Alec nodded. "Agreed. They wouldn't have known

what they were a few thousand years ago. But we know now."

"And they're not werewolves?" Kole asked again. "What's the difference between a werewolf and a lycan?"

"Werewolves are believed to change involuntarily with the phases of the moon," Jodis answered. "Lycan, on the other hand, have the ability to decide when they will shift into wolf form."

"So they're shape-shifters?" Kole clarified. His brow creased, clearly confused by the whole thing. "They wore human skin?"

"We don't know anything about the Zoan as a race or breed." Cronin answered this time. "They are not known to us at all. But from what we've seen from Alec's memories, it appears they have a human exterior, if you will, but are a lycan underneath. I would assume they can shift to either form at will. It would explain how they've remained undetected all this time."

Eleanor spoke next. "They called themselves vukodlak as well. Meaning vampire wolf. Which is what? A breed of lycan?"

"If a blood drinking wolf can be defined as a lycan, then theoretically, yes," Cronin replied.

Alec finished writing down the points of interest. "But what I saw, what I showed you, what do you make of that? They looked—"

"Threatening," Eiji replied. "I fear to see them again, and fear is not something I have felt in a long, long time."

"Under their skin they looked like wolves," Cronin stated. "Misshapen, somewhat human, grotesque. So many sharp teeth. But they looked like something else. Scaly? Like a sharp-toothed lizard almost?"

"They're militarized," Alec said. "They stood in formation. They have a leader. That at least tells us they have a hierarchy and a militia mindset. It's something, at least."

"And their clothes," Eleanor said. "Cloaks. I can't see what they're hiding underneath them."

"And what of their abilities?" Eiji asked. "They can appear in Alec's mind telepathically. Then they appear here physically but only to him? What kind of talent is that?"

"And if they have the talent, why doesn't Alec?" Jodis added her own unanswerable question.

"And of the lapse in time?" Cronin asked. "We all saw that. Alec spoke with them while we stood still, frozen. It was as though they stopped time for the world, except for themselves and Alec."

It was a human habit that made Alec check his watch, only to find the hands were not moving. He tapped it, and nothing. It was the expensive watch Cronin had bought him from Tokyo just over a year ago, surely the battery wasn't dead....

"Alec?" Cronin asked, looking at Alec's watch.

"It's stopped. Could be a coincidence," he said, though he knew it wasn't.

"When did it stop?" Eiji asked.

He glanced at the clock on the wall, though his sense of time was perfect. "Forty-seven minutes ago."

"About the time the Zoan appeared in the living room," Jodis noted.

"Not about," Alec corrected her gently. "*Exactly* the time they appeared. They really did stop time."

They sat in silence for a while, as everyone took in what that meant. It was hard to fathom. Kole shook his head. "But you didn't stop with the rest of us," he said. "And that worries me."

Alec shivered, something he'd not done since his vampire change. "Which means when they come for me, I'm on my own."

Cronin started to growl. It was a low menacing sound and he didn't seem to even know he was doing it.

"I don't like it either," Alec confessed, looking directly at Cronin. Then he glanced around at the others. "It appears that I have no powers over them. I tried to immobilize them and to shield the others, but nothing worked."

"So in this—" Eiji paused, and Alec saw him searching his mind for the right word. "—time slip, you're powerless?"

"I think so," Alec admitted. "Though I'd need another encounter to test it for certain. I was taken off-guard before, but now I'll know what to expect."

Cronin's growl got louder. "Another encounter? Alec, you say such a thing as though you look forward to it."

"Actually," Alec said, trying to remain calm, "as you'll recall, I didn't have any choice in it. It would appear that if the Zoan wish to speak to me, then they will, regardless if I want them to or not."

"And this concerns me the most," Cronin replied. He walked over to Alec and rested his forehead on Alec's chin. "I apologize for my tone, Alec. I know you don't wish for such things, but the idea of you facing them alone... now they've declared their hand as your enemy...."

"I know," Alec agreed quietly. He cupped Cronin's face and kissed the side of his head.

Cronin murmured, sounding defeated already. "There has to be someone. Someone somewhere who knows of such things! How has this escaped us? Why are we only learning of such ancient creatures now?"

"That's what we need to find out," Alec said. "We need to work on the who, what, how, and why. We need to try and look behind them to see who sent them or where they're from, and most importantly, what they want. That's how we beat them. Find their weak spot."

Eiji grinned and clapped his hands together. "I love it when you talk like that, Alec." Cronin huffed and glared at Eiji, but he wasn't deterred. In fact he laughed. "What? I can't help it. When Alec does his policing thing"—Eiji waved his hand at the whiteboard—"adventure and mayhem usually follow."

Alec smiled at him, then looked to Jacques, Eleanor, and Kole. "Eiji, Jodis, Cronin, and I will be leaving for a short time. There's someone I need to speak to." Then Alec looked to Jacques again. "Can I ask one thing?"

"Of course," he replied.

"Look into gargoyles," Alec said. "I don't know why. When I first saw them, that word came to me. It was not a name they gave me, but something in my mind thought it. Research what you can."

"Gargoyles?" Cronin asked.

Alec nodded with a shrug. "I know it's weird. But seriously, vampire mummies in Egypt, terracotta vampires in China.... Nothing trips my weird-shit-o-meter anymore."

"Where are we going?" Jodis asked.

"To see Jorge," Alec answered.

Eleanor shook her head. "Alec, your talent far surpasses his. If you can't see the Zoan, no one can."

"Not Jorge himself," Alec clarified. "But the vampire dead. He speaks with them. I do not. I can see them in his mind, like a window, but only he has that power." He shrugged at all the vampires looking at him. "Maybe if there isn't a vampire alive who knows about the Zoan, maybe there's one that's dead who does."

CHAPTER FOUR

ALEC MADE a small detour first to bring Jorge a gift. He'd seen him a few times in the last twelve months, and every time he brought along a small token of thanks. Alec understood Jorge so much better now that he could see into his mind. He knew the voices he spoke were often not his own. Vampires all over the world had assumed Jorge was afflicted with multiple personalities or dissociative identity disorder, as it was called these days.

But it wasn't that at all.

Jorge had a mental window to the dead. Vampire dead, to be exact. Something they'd learned only when Alec's dead mother spoke to them when Alec was changed into a vampire.

The voice Jorge spoke with was his, but in his mind, Alec could see the dead vampire talking. Jorge was, for all intents and purposes, a portal to the vampire afterlife.

And what's more, Alec liked the kid. Misunderstood for a hundred years, but still just a five-year-old boy, Jorge had been paramount to Alec's survival and transformation from human to vampire. Jorge had been abducted from his humble hut in the jungles of Bolivia and used as bait to lure Alec to China by Rilind, a vengeful Illyrian vampire who wanted to use Alec's powers. When Alec and Cronin had returned Jorge safe and well, it was then Alec realized the distraught Adelmo, the man who looked after Jorge, was a *father* to Jorge. He wasn't a caregiver, or baby-sitter, like some of the rumors Alec had heard. He was, by vampire bond, the child's father figure.

Alec could see it. He could see the bond between fated couples, like a tethering of souls. And not all bonds were for couples, or so Alec had tried to explain. Some bonds were to be family. Like Adelmo and Jorge. If Alec lived for a thousand years, he'd never forget the moment they took Jorge back to Adelmo, how the little boy ran to him, and how Adelmo scooped him up and cried tears of joy and relief.

Adelmo and Jorge lived a humble life: a small hut, sparse but practical furniture, no electricity, with no comforts of the twenty-first century that Alec took for granted. They were happy that way. But a gift was warranted. Every time they visited—Jorge had only left his jungle home once since the ordeal in China, and that was for Alec's and Cronin's wedding—Alec took him something small but special.

The first time it was a new watch, after the one Alec had given him the very first time they'd met, was taken. The second time it was a box of books, both reading and coloring, with the biggest box of crayons and markers Alec could find. Considering Jorge's talents and his vampire age of over one hundred years, the others had thought it stupid. But Jorge was so excited, and Adelmo was most grateful.

This visit Alec had decided a new soccer ball was in order. He'd leapt Cronin, Eiji, and Jodis to the back alley behind a major retailer of sporting goods in Sucre, Bolivia's capital. It was evening and the store was full of late night shoppers. While Alec collected what he wanted and stood in the long line to be served, Cronin, Eiji, and Jodis went off to the side waiting. Rather impatiently.

Granted, Alec had become rather accustomed to the not-waiting that leaping brought with it, but he wanted to do this right. Yes, he could leap to any store anywhere in the world and take what he wanted, or leap it to him without having to go anywhere, but a gift should be chosen and purchased.

Much to Eiji's displeasure. He hadn't stopped grumbling to himself yet.

Quit your whining, Alec told Eiji in his mind.

Eiji glared at him. *Alec,* he retorted sharply. *A group of unknown creatures threatened your life merely hours ago. I don't think it's wise or funny that we risk a public outing to buy a child's soccer ball. Could you not have just taken it?*

Do we not take enough from mankind? Alec replied.

An image of himself feeding flashed through Eiji's mind, so Alec knew Eiji understood what he meant. He pouted. *Great. A vampire with a conscience. Perhaps you could have chosen a store that was not so busy.*

Alec looked at Jodis and allowed himself to speak in her mind. *How do you put up with the constant whining?*

Jodis only smiled.

Eiji shot her a look. "What did he say to you just now?"

She lied terribly. "Nothing."

Eiji stared at her for a long second. "Yes, he did." He turned back to Alec. "Yes you did." Then back to Jodis. "Why did you say he didn't? Why did you lie to me?"

Cronin chuckled. "Alec, do you think perhaps you could hurry things along. Waiting in service lines is not something we're accustomed to."

"Waiting for anything, really," Eiji added.

"For someone who's as old as you, I'd have thought you'd have acquired some patience," Alec said with a laugh.

But he was right. People were starting to stare. In a store where the clientele and staff were predominately South American, men were starting to notice Jodis—with her porcelain skin, long white hair, and breathtaking beauty. Eiji was just as striking, with his Japanese features of high cheekbones and long black hair, but the two of them together looked like a freakin' commercial for perfection. Not entirely a human beauty, but striking nonetheless.

And Cronin... well, Alec couldn't even begin to quantify how attractive he was.

"*Disculpe, señor,*" a woman's voice called out. Alec looked up to see the sales assistant smiling expectantly at him, waiting for him to come to the counter. Alec made the transaction despite the woman's thought processes to-ing and fro-ing between finding him hot and finding him frightening. She knew something wasn't quite right—or even human. She considered then dismissed the idea as foolish. She still wasn't too sure when she handed him his purchases.

"*Tenga un buen dia,*" Alec replied smoothly, telling her to have a nice day. He gave his voice a touch of huskiness and added his flirty eyes. The woman stammered her thanks, though Alec could hear Cronin grind his teeth over the sound of the woman's giggles.

He grinned as he walked out of the store. "What?" Alec replied to Cronin's glare. "She couldn't decide if we were ridiculously sexy or an inhuman threat. I went with the sexy option."

Cronin huffed as they walked along the sidewalk. "I'd have preferred you not flirt with her. A woman, no less."

Jodis scoffed. "Something wrong with being a woman?"

"No, no," Cronin amended. "That was not my intention. It's just that—"

Alec laughed and slipped his arm through Jodis' and walked ahead with her, leaving a smiling Eiji and a pouting Cronin to walk behind. They turned into the dark alley they'd arrived in and when they were completely shrouded in darkness, Alec dropped Jodis' arm and kissed Cronin until he smiled.

Eiji only sighed three times.

When they finally broke apart, Alec laughed before he leapt them to the now familiar hut in the Rurrenabaque jungle.

"ALEC!" Jorge cried, running and jumping into his open arms. Alec hugged the vampire child, before putting him back on his own two feet and ruffled the boy's hair. "What you got for Jorge this time?"

Adelmo hushed him. "Jorge! Manners." But Adelmo smiled regardless.

Cronin liked that Jorge and Alec had become friends, and Adelmo too. And Cronin would be forever in Jorge's debt for saving Alec when they were in China.

Adelmo graciously welcomed them into his home, and they looked on while Jorge opened the bag from the sporting goods store. He was so excited for his brand new soccer ball, a pair of new soccer cleats, and a shirt with the name Pelé on the back.

Needless to say, Jorge was incredibly excited. He jumped and clapped, saying things like, "We are so happy. Jorge is so happy. Alec is good friend."

All Alec could do was laugh.

Cronin likened Alec to be Jorge's favorite uncle. He even did up the laces in the cleats for him, then of course, they went into the clearing and played a game of one-on-one.

This was their third trip to the Amazonian jungle in twelve months, since China, and the second trip that Eiji and Jodis had accompanied them on.

"I take it not all is well," Adelmo started.

Cronin shook his head. "There have been developments."

"Has Jorge said anything?" Eiji asked.

Adelmo shook his head. "Not anything alarming. Nothing new."

"A group has presented themselves to Alec, and only to Alec. We cannot see them. They've declared themselves his enemy."

Adelmo gasped, and hearing the conversation, Jorge stopped playing soccer. He looked up at Alec, the game seemingly forgotten. "Enemy to the key?"

Alec picked up the soccer ball and sighed. He ruffled Jorge's hair again. "Yep. Apparently."

"Jorge not like it," Jorge said. His face had grown dark, angry, and he scowled. "Alec is our friend."

Alec stared at the little boy. "Have you seen anything?"

Cronin wasn't sure if Alec was asking Jorge himself or asking the vampire he saw in Jorge's mind.

Jorge shook his head. "No."

"They call themselves The Zoan," Alec said. If he was expecting an immediate reaction, he didn't get one.

Nothing.

Jorge stood still, his face neutral, his eyes completely

black, and Cronin knew then that Alec was talking to the vampire he could see in Jorge's mind.

After a moment, Alec nodded. "Very well. Thank you."

Jorge blinked his eyes back to normal and shook his head. "What is a Zoan?"

Alec shrugged. "I was kinda hoping you could tell me." Then he looked at Cronin, Eiji, and Jodis. "They're getting someone who can help. Who knew that heaven had a call center?"

"They're *getting someone*?" Eiji asked incredulously. "What does that mean?"

"Well, she used the words 'call forth,' but if I said that, I'd sound like a pompous ass," Alec said. Eiji laughed.

"Who did you speak to?" Cronin asked.

"Heather. My mother," Alec answered. "She seems to be on speed dial or something."

Jorge looked confused, obviously not familiar with modern technologies. "She links to you. If you need her, she answers," he said. His chubby cheeks heated pink. "Jorge like her."

Jorge must have thought something next, because Alec answered. "She is pretty," he agreed. "But not as pretty as me."

Jorge laughed, and snatched the ball from Alec and kicked a winning goal between the two trees marked as posts.

Cronin smiled as he watched them play, but something Jorge said had stuck with him. When they'd gone inside and were seated around the table, Cronin brought it up again.

"Jorge, before you said that you liked Alec's mother?"

"She's nice to Jorge," he replied.

That's what Cronin thought he meant. "Are there people there that are not nice to Jorge?"

Jorge's face darkened a fraction. "Jorge doesn't like some things they show. Not all things make Jorge happy."

Cronin recalled how Jorge had seen visions of the starving vampire mummies in Egypt being slaughtered. "No, I presume not. But the people there are nice to you?"

Jorge nodded.

Cronin smiled at him but pressed on with his questions. "Are there a lot of people there?"

Jorge half nodded, half shrugged. "Jorge doesn't see them all. Just those who want Jorge to see them."

Cronin, Alec's voice sounded in Cronin's mind. *Are you okay?*

Cronin knew Alec would see why he was asking such things. He looked to him and gave a nod. *Of course.*

I didn't mean to pry, Alec went on. *But your mind is the clearest to me. Your thoughts are pretty loud right now. Can we talk about this later?*

Before Cronin could reply, Alec spun to face Jorge. Apparently whoever they were going to find with information on the Zoan had returned because Jorge's eyes were all black again. Alec smiled at Jorge. "It's Johan! I can see Johan!"

Johan was the vampire who had died protecting Cronin when they'd fought in Egypt. Cronin had known him for many years, and although Johan made his affection toward Cronin known, Cronin had respectfully declined his advances. They'd remained friends. Johan—a talented cartographer—had drawn the maps of the Great Pyramid tunnels for them and had died in battle against Queen Keket's Illyrian guards.

He'd taken a wooden bullet to the heart so Cronin could live.

"It's good to see you again," Alec said, staring at Jorge.

"You're happy. I can see it."

"And you make quite the vampire, Alec," Johan replied through Jorge. It took some getting used to, watching Jorge speak for someone else, as though he was possessed. "We always knew you were special."

Alec smiled fondly at him. "I owe you an immeasurable debt, Johan. You sacrificed yourself to protect Cronin, and that will not ever be forgotten."

"But I am happier here than I ever was in all my years there," Johan said.

"You met your fated one," Alec said. "I can see the bond."

Jorge nodded his little head. "And it is he who knows the information you seek."

"Can I show Cronin, Eiji, and Jodis?" Alec asked. "I can let them see what I see, if that's okay with you."

Jorge smiled and gave a nod. "Very well. I have a feeling Cronin will want to see."

Cronin was unnerved by what Jorge was saying on behalf of Johan. "See what?"

Then an image flashed in his mind and he could see Johan; Alec had given everyone the gift of seeing what he saw. Johan was just as Cronin remembered him, though Alec was right; he did look happier.

The background was unclear, and exactly where Johan was standing was a mystery, but he held out his hand and another man joined him.

Cronin couldn't believe what he saw.

"Cronin," a familiar but long-forgotten voice said. "It is good to see you again, my old friend."

A face Cronin had not seen in seven hundred years. The only other lover he had ever known.

Willem.

CHAPTER FIVE

THE ONLY OTHER man Cronin had ever bedded now stood in front of Alec, in Jorge's mind. He was a roguish-looking guy with a sparkle in his blue eyes. He had blond hair, a wide forehead, and a strong jaw. He was handsome, no doubt about it, and Alec felt a pang of jealousy twist in his belly.

He contained his emotions, so the others wouldn't know he felt that way. He could have let it seep from him like an angry mist and crawl over their skin the way it seemed to crawl over his, but Alec controlled it well.

"Willem?" Cronin said. "It is a surprise to see you, I will admit. Though a pleasure, all the same."

Alec's jealousy bubbled a little bit more.

"And you, my friend." Willem looked at Eiji and Jodis. "You keep the same company, I see, Cronin," he said with a smile. "Eiji, Jodis, time has kept you well."

"And you," Jodis replied.

Willem bowed his head a little, and when he looked up again, he looked straight at Cronin. "Ah, Cronin. Fate has chosen well for you. The key, and I would expect nothing less for you, my friend."

Cronin stepped closer to Alec so he could put his arm around him. "Willem, this is Alec. Alec, my old friend Willem."

Alec forced a tight smile. "Cronin has told me about you. Nice to meet you."

"And Johan," Cronin bowed his head. "I am so very pleased to see you once again. I owe you my life."

Johan smiled warmly. "It was my fate," he said simply. "I didn't know it at the time, but I had to leave your world to meet my fated one. He was waiting for me."

"Fate is an incongruous, ironical thing, is it not?" Willem asked rhetorically. "That my Johan and I both knew you, Cronin."

Cronin tightened his hold on Alec. "Fate is a curious thing indeed."

"You look well, Cronin," Willem said. "There is a light in your eyes that was absent when I knew you. A light I assume we can thank Alec for."

Alec hated that this man, this ex-lover, had a history with Cronin. Hated that he'd touched him in the most intimate of ways. Hated that they'd seen the world at a different time. Hated that Alec would never have that.

It was an irrational feeling; the vampire was dead, living on some ethereal plane. Hell, he was even fated to someone else. But still, Alec couldn't help the way he felt. Regardless of how much he confined the emotion, it was still there.

"The Zoan?" Alec asked, probably sounding more abrupt than what would be considered polite. He didn't care. He needed this to be over. "You know of them?"

Willem tried not to smile, as though he could read

Alec's mind. Maybe he could, Alec reasoned. He still didn't care.

"I know of them," he replied. "I've not seen them with my own eyes, but I am familiar with their kind."

"Who are they?" Jodis quickly asked. "Where do they come from?"

"And why have we not heard of them?" Eiji added.

"They are, as their name suggests, *zoanthropes*. They are known to humans as many names. Lycan, *chimera*, or *therianthropes*. Though humans believe it is a psychosis where the person can change into another animal. That's not quite correct. Zoan are creatures who can change into a human. They shape-shift, for the want of a layman term. But their true form is not human."

"So they have many names?" Alec asked.

"Yes," Willem clarified. "In the same way a human does. Human, Homo Sapien, American, English, Caucasian. The list is long."

"So lycan and chimera are the same thing," Alec repeated, more to himself than anyone else.

"Chimera, by human definition, is a hybrid creature," Willem said. "Forget human definitions and misconceptions, Alec. They are close but not exact. Humans confuse mythology and fact. What they choose to believe as myth and folklore quite often is the truth, but that truth is horrific and frequently unexplainable, so they choose to paint it as a fairytale."

"Yes, we know," Jodis agreed kindly.

"Why now?" Alec asked. "And why have we only heard of these creatures *now*?"

Cronin didn't wait for Willem to reply. "What do these Zoan want with Alec?"

"I would imagine they want his power," Willem said

bluntly. "Alec, when you were changed there was a great shift in energy. The Callanish Stones created a vortex of immense power, the circle of light, if you'll recall."

"What of it?" Cronin pressed.

"Well, there was an equally powerful but opposite effect," Willem told them. "It seemed to open a portal."

"A portal?" Alec snorted. "Oh, good. I've seen this movie. Great big mechanical worms fly in and destroy the world."

"Not mechanical worms," Willem corrected, like he'd missed the joke all together. "Zoans. There was an energy flux in Göbekli Tepe, Turkey. The oldest circle of stones on earth."

"They came through a portal?" Alec repeated. "For real?"

Willem chuckled. "I like him, Cronin."

Alec growled. "Wait a goddamned minute. Look, I appreciate your help and all, but mystical creatures from *portals*?"

Johan put his hand up. "Alec, is it no more incredible than mummified vampires or terracotta vampires?"

Alec sighed. "Johan, your logic is doing my head in right now. Please stop it."

Johan laughed. "You have not changed, my friend. So do what you do best. Put the pieces together so you can see the bigger picture. Do your detective thing."

Willem gave Johan an adoring squeeze. It should have pleased Alec to see him being affectionate with his fated one, but it didn't. He was jealous and petty, and he didn't care.

"The Göbekli Tepe circle of stones dates back to prehistory," Willem went on to say. He seemed impervious to Alec's mood. "So these creatures are *old*, Alec. Every so often, the Zoan is believed to have appeared but only from portals in newer standing stones."

Alec was tired of the riddles. "What does that even mean?"

Willem wasn't smiling now. "To come from the oldest portal on the planet, I would assume these are the oldest Zoan. The most powerful."

Alec put his hands through his hair and sighed. "How do they stop time?"

"I do not know."

"Why do I have no powers over them?"

Willem answered quietly. "I do not know. I would assume it is the time differential that inhibits your abilities. That your talents, in multitudes as they are, simply do not exist on that plane."

"How do we fight them?" Cronin asked.

When Willem didn't answer, Alec rephrased the question. "Do I win? Or do I die?"

Willem frowned. "That I cannot tell you."

"Or you won't," Alec quipped back.

"I cannot," he replied simply. "For I do not know."

"But you can see them?" Alec kept on. "When they show themselves to me? You can see that, wherever it is you are?"

Willem gave a nod. "Yes. We see most everything." Then he smiled sadly. "I see pits of fire, Alec. That is all. The Zoan breathe it."

"They breathe fire?" Eiji asked, his voice almost an octave higher.

Willem gave a nod. "I would assume it is from where the myth of the dragon stems. A hybrid creature of bird and lizard, if you will."

Alec snorted out a laugh, quickly becoming overwhelmed with this incredible information. "Dragons? Like Puff, The Magic Fucking Dragon?"

Willem didn't smile. "Have you not yet learned that human histories are not what they seem, Alec? Can you not see that, in the great expanse that is your mind? You need to let go of the human delusion, Alec."

Alec didn't reply to that. Instead, he just said, "Jorge has grown tired. Let the boy rest."

"Wait!" Cronin said, stopping them before they disappeared. He looked right at Willem. "Where are you?"

Willem just smiled beautifully, waved his hand, and they were gone.

Jorge's eyes went back to normal and he fell forward. Everyone moved to catch him, but Alec was the quickest and caught him easily. "Whoa there, little guy," he said, sitting him on a chair. "You okay, Jorge? You scared me."

Jorge nodded weakly. "Jorge tired."

"I'm sorry it took longer than I expected," Alec said, putting his palm to Jorge's chest. "You are weak. Can you feel me making you better?"

Jorge nodded and gave him a full smile; his little fangs peeked out of his lips, and Alec couldn't believe he once found that alarming. Now he thought it was cute. Jorge laughed. "Alec fix Jorge."

Alec ruffled Jorge's hair. "Any time, kiddo." When he was sure Jorge was okay, Alec stood up to full height. "Well, that meeting was interesting." He glared at Cronin. "And not exactly unwelcome by some."

Cronin was taken aback. He shook his head. "What?"

Your ex-boyfriend was happy to see you too.

Cronin blanched. "No, no. Alec, you misread my curiosity."

Alec took a deep breath and his nostrils flared. The irrational—stupidly irrational—anger wouldn't dissipate. "I need to leave," Alec said as quietly as he could. He needed to leave because he really wanted to expel a fuckton of rage and he figured Adelmo and Jorge didn't want their little pocket of the Amazon wiped off the map.

Cronin put up his hand, palm forward. "Be calm, m'cridhe. I will take Jodis and Eiji back to New York and be back in just a moment. I will go with you."

Cronin looked concerned and a little lost at Alec's emotional outburst, and that only served to layer guilt on top of Alec's anger. Kind of similar to what gasoline does to fire.

In the blink of an eye, Cronin was gone along with Eiji and Jodis. Alec knew he'd owe them an apology, another one, and that burned in him as well. Alec leaned down so he was eye level with Jorge. "I am very grateful for you." Then he looked up at Adelmo. "And you, Adelmo."

Cronin reappeared and he seemed relieved to see Alec was still there. And again, more guilt poured onto the blazing fire that Alec was struggling to contain. He couldn't even look Cronin in the eye, and that hurt the most.

Alec gave Jorge the best smile he could muster. "If you need me, for anything, just call me in your mind. I'll hear it. I'll be listening for you, okay?"

They said their good-byes and Alec leapt himself and Cronin to the most remote place he could think of. Somewhere he could scream and detonate bombs of rage without being seen or heard by humans.

Antarctica blizzards, or whiteouts, were loud. Something Alec didn't realize before now, though he was pleased. The winter, dark and freezing cold, seemed perfectly apt for his mood. And even though the snow blasted him from all directions, he could feel the earth beneath his shoes, and it grounded him. He let the wrath and jealousy that bubbled in his chest boil over. He let his head fall back and he roared, sending flurries of snow rippling out from him.

Cronin stood four feet in front of him, almost whited out with snow, but he never took his eyes off Alec. He spoke in his normal voice, and even over the rumbling blizzard, Alec heard him just fine. "Alec, tell me what angers you so?"

"Everything!" he bellowed. He clenched his fists and roared as he smashed the ground with every ounce of strength he had. A creaking fissure split the ice beneath his punch. "Why was he there? Willem," Alec said the name as though it tasted bitter on his tongue. "You were pleased to see him."

"He was a friend," Cronin said. "An acquaintance with similar inclinations. Nothing more."

"You slept with him!"

"Yes! Out of curiosity. I'd never experienced such things before!" Cronin shook his head. He was angry in return now. "This cannot be what angers you, Alec. You've known about Willem since we first met. Have I ever questioned those that have seen your bed before me?"

"Yes!" Alec replied petulantly. "You wanted to kill them, remember?"

"I said that in jest, Alec. And to what end does this worry you? You cannot change what is done!"

"You chose him!" Alec cried. "You never chose me!" He regretted his choice of words immediately and felt the resulting stab of hurt in Cronin's chest.

"Were my words at our wedding not enough for you?" Cronin asked. His anger gone, replaced by hurt.

Alec pushed out a bloom of sorry so Cronin could feel just how bad Alec felt. "Of course they were enough," he said. "They were everything. Cronin, I can't explain why I feel this way. It's not rational, but I can't seem to stop it. I don't blame you, and I don't blame him. I know you would choose me if fate had not done so already."

"You're dealing with a constant heavy burden, Alec. Don't add an unnecessary weight."

"Don't make excuses for me," Alec whispered against the blizzard. "I was an ass."

Cronin smiled and finally closed the distance between them. He put his hand to Alec's face. "Don't talk that way about the man who holds my heart."

Alec took a deep breath as though Cronin's words lightened the heaviness in his chest. "He was handsome," Alec allowed.

Cronin laughed like snow wasn't pounding against him. "Don't think for one moment he even compares to you. Like a candle to the sun, Alec. There is no comparison. Though I am pleased he found his fated one. And Johan, of all people! They deserve the happiness they've found in each other, don't you think?"

Alec nodded, but he knew he had to confess what was truly troubling him. "I worry this new war is one I cannot win," Alec finally admitted. "I worry for the pain it will cause you if I were to die."

Cronin brushed the snow from Alec's hair and the side of his face, though it was only replaced afresh not half a second later. "Oh, Alec. Fear not, m'cridhe. I would follow you through this life and the next."

"Is that what you were curious about? In the hut?" Alec asked. "At first I thought you were just interested because it was... *him*. But it's more than that, isn't it." It wasn't a question. "It's the whole afterlife thing."

"Alec, cast Willem from your mind. Think only of us

and no more of him. But before I answer your question, do you think we might seek a more hospitable location?" Cronin paused as a squall of snow hammered them both from the side.

Alec had barely nodded before Cronin put his hand to his arm and leapt them. The warm night air in Johannesburg was a startling change. Melting fast, clumps of snow fell off them onto the dirt alleys of the Diepsloot slums and puddles of water quickly pooled at their feet.

Alec was instantly bombarded with a few hundred thousand voices in his head before he shut them out. He knew why Cronin had chosen this place: he wanted to feed.

Cronin shook himself off, much like a dog, and it made Alec laugh. He did the same, but he was still drenched through. "Maybe Antarctica wasn't the best idea I've ever had."

Cronin snorted. "Well, you'll certainly give the geologists and climate change experts something to talk about. That crack in the middle of the continent will have them scratching their heads for a time, I'm sure."

"It felt good to punch something that hard," Alec admitted.

"It was magnificent to witness."

"I'm sorry if my anger took you by surprise," Alec said.

"I cannot lie and say that I don't find your jealousy appealing," Cronin said with a sly smile. "I rather like seeing you get possessive of me."

Alec snorted at that. "If I could have reached through Jorge's mind, I would have ripped Willem's head from his body." He shrugged. "I'm sure he's a nice guy and all, but he's done things with you that—"

Cronin put his finger to Alec's lips. "Think no more of him."

"I'm sorry I let my jealousy and pride come before you."

"Think no more of it, m'cridhe. You don't owe me an explanation or apology."

Well, that wasn't true, but before Alec could argue, Cronin spoke again. "Can I ask you something?"

"Of course."

"It's about what you see when you look into Jorge's mind. Can you see where they are?"

Alec shook his head. "Nothing specific. The whole concept of there being an afterlife is fascinating to you, isn't it?"

"How can it not be?" Cronin countered. "To even consider that there is such a thing for us—" He shook his head in wonder. "—a heaven! For us!"

Truth be told, Alec hadn't given heaven much credence. Not as a human and certainly not as a vampire. He wasn't a religious man, so the notion of heaven and hell fell by the wayside. But it was clearly something Cronin prized.

"A heaven or next life," Alec amended. "I don't know what or where it is exactly. I can't see details of their surroundings."

Alec could feel the undercurrent of peace it gave Cronin, to know there was more to life, even if this one were to end. "It confounds me to consider our own mortality," Cronin said. "We are granted *im*mortality in this life, yet here we are faced with a hereafter. It baffles me."

"Do you think you're not deserving?"

"Well, in leaving behind my humanity, I also left behind a mindfulness for human life."

"That's not true," Alec said. "You respect human life. You only take what you need to feed. You don't kill them for entertainment or sport."

Cronin shrugged one shoulder. "True."

"Why the consciousness for such things now?" Alec asked. "You've lived a long time to only just realize this."

Cronin let out a deep breath. "I've never been faced with the possibility of there being something more."

"And yet, even when you thought all faith was lost, you still acted with a kindness toward humans." Alec put his hand to Cronin's chest. "That proves what kind of heart you have."

Cronin shrugged again, but before he could speak, Alec's head turned to the sound of different voices. He heard the mental voices before the auditory ones. Two men working as a team. One of them was warring between fight and flight, too scared to do either. And the other man, the leader of the two, was holding a small child but worried that the woman's screams would cause too much attention. *Shut her up, shut her up*, he kept saying, out loud and in his head. The first man finally closed his fist and took a step toward the stricken woman, who'd been knocked to the floor.

"Be ready to take the child," Alec whispered before leaping them both to where the scene was unfolding. Alec grabbed the two men by the throats before they could blink, strangling their screams of surprise and fear.

Cronin quickly and carefully took the wailing child from the man's arms before he could drop her. The woman on the ground cried out, her eyes wide with fear, as she scrambled backwards away from them. But Cronin held out her little girl, no more than eighteen months old, and gently handed her back to the woman. "Take her. Be safe," Cronin said. "These two men will not bother you anymore." And the woman scrambled out of the shack, her baby safe in her arms.

Alec snarled at the two men. Their feet kicked in mid-air, their hands were uselessly trying to release Alec's grip on their necks. "I know what you wanted to do to the baby," he snarled at them, his fangs bared. "You sick fucks. There's a special place in hell for people like you."

The men both struggled. One of them tried punching Alec, swiping his fists blindly at him. It hurt Alec no more than a newborn kitten would, though Cronin clearly didn't like the fact the man was hitting him. He took him from Alec, the man's arms now swinging even wilder, his eyes bulging with a new kind of fear.

Cronin bowed his head to Alec. "Thank you, my love."

"Any time," Alec replied. "I happen to like taking you out for dinner."

The man Cronin was holding pissed his pants. Cronin sighed. "I hate when they do that."

"I hate humans who do unspeakable things to children," Alec said, turning his attention back to the struggling man. Alec saw memory after memory in the man's mind of the horrific things he'd done. If it were possible for Alec to vomit, he would have. "I hope whatever meets you on the other side does to you what you've done to them." The man struggled some more before Alec twisted his wrist just so and snapped the man's neck. He put his teeth to his throat and fed.

When they were done, before Alec could drop the disgusting human to the muddy floor, Cronin said, "Hold onto him. There's something I want to show you."

ALEC WAS SURPRISED when Cronin leapt them to the savannah plains. The Tanzanian landscape was not what he was expecting at all. He could see by the color of the horizon that the sun would be up in about an hour.

"I've never brought anyone else here," Cronin said softly. "Though I've been coming here for many years."

"Why are you just bringing me here now?" Alec asked. "It's beautiful."

Cronin smiled and dumped the body into the dirt. "Don't be alarmed."

Alec let the body he was holding fall to the ground as well. "Don't be alarmed about what?"

With a smug smirk, Cronin let out a bellowing roar. It was a sound Alec had never heard him make before. Then in the distance, Alec heard it. First it was the sound of feet—big feet—padding on dirt at a gallop, then he heard the beating heart.

Then he saw it.

The male lion raced toward them, and even though Alec's place was now at the top of the food chain, he still took a reflexive step back. "Jesus Christ."

Cronin just grinned as the lion's pace became a swaggering walk as he came in to meet them. "It's been a while since I've paid you a visit, old friend," Cronin said, scratching the lion's forehead. "I brought someone with me this time," Cronin said to the lion. "He is my husband. I thought it was about time he met you."

Alec couldn't believe it. "Um, so when you said that time you were off feeding the lions of Tanzania, you weren't joking?"

Still grinning, Cronin shook his head. "No. I've fed this pride for generations, discarding evidence." Cronin nodded toward the lion. "Put your hand out. He will smell you."

Alec had never imagined standing this close to a wild lion. But, like all felines, lions were drawn to vampires. These were just... the biggest felines of all.

The lion sniffed Alec's hand and started to purr, a loud

rumbling sound. It nudged his hip with its forehead, and if he'd still been human, it would have knocked him off his feet. Only after Alec had scratched the lion's forehead, did it seem interested in the meal they'd brought it. Then, the rest of the pride turned up for the left overs. The rest of the lions, the females and cubs, all swarmed around Alec, rubbing against him and purring.

"Well, they've never done that to me," Cronin smiled as he looked on. "I think they like you."

Alec couldn't believe his eyes. He couldn't believe Cronin had done this for years, and he couldn't believe he was only learning about it now. This was something he'd never shown Willem....

He looked at his husband and shook his head in wonder. "And you thought you didn't deserve heaven."

Cronin gave him a smile that put the beauty of the African savannah to shame.

CHAPTER SIX

ALEC WAS in a much better mood when they arrived back at the New York City apartment. The first thing he did was apologize to Jodis and Eiji. "I acted like an ass," he said. Alec preferred to apologize out loud, not directly into the minds of the people he'd wronged. It wasn't always possible, like earlier with Jodis, but he still preferred to speak the words aloud. It wasn't in his nature to be arrogant about such things. Just because he had powers—all the known powers in vampire history, except for Jorge's—didn't mean he wasn't man enough to admit he was wrong.

And just because Alec was the most powerful vampire in the world didn't mean Eiji wouldn't take the piss out of him. He laughed at Alec. "I think you can probably take Willem off your Christmas card list."

Alec grumbled. "Oh, hardy har."

Jodis fought a smile. "It was a surprise to see him," she said, eyeing Cronin. "To no one more so, than you."

"It was a surprise," Cronin conceded. "And to see Willem happy with Johan, even more so. A fating well-deserved, I think."

"Agreed." Jodis gave a knowing smirk. "He waited even longer than you."

"And I guess I'll need to apologize to him too," Alec said, rolling his eyes. He tried not to sound petulant and failed dismally. "If I ever see him again."

Eiji chuckled to himself. "Oh Alec, you and Willem have a lot in common."

Alec snarled, and Cronin put his hand up. "A change of subject, perhaps?" He shot Eiji a glare. "Deliberately antagonizing the most powerful vampire on the planet is not conducive to your longevity, Eiji. Or to the foundations of this building. There's now a healthy crack in the Antarctic ice sheet down to the tectonic plate to prove my point."

Alec just shrugged which made Eiji laugh some more, not fazed at all.

Jodis shook her head at him. "Speaking of painful deaths, is it not amazing that there is some world after this one?" Her blue eyes danced with excitement.

"Yes!" Cronin cried. "I tried to explain my excitement of this to Alec." He and Jodis went on to talk of heaven and what it could possibly mean, but Alec left them to it.

"You really put a crack in the south pole?" Eiji asked him.

"Chile and Argentina are probably experiencing tsunamis as we speak." Alec sighed. "I was angry. Figured it was the safest place to let off some steam."

"You're not angry now, though," Eiji noted.

"No, Cronin took me someplace magical."

Eiji put his hand up like he was stopping traffic. "Stop. I don't need to hear about that."

Alec laughed. "Not that kind of magical. But now that you mention it," he turned to the direction Cronin had gone. "That's a really good idea."

Jacques interrupted. He was holding a book written in Latin. "Alec, a moment?"

So much for sex. "Of course."

"You asked us to research gargoyles," he said. "I think I've found something."

"What is it?" Alec asked, looking at the pages of the open book he was holding.

"The word gargoyle is derivative of the French *gargouille,* which means pipe or throat, or the Spanish *gargola,* for the sound of water. They are believed to be a construction device to divert rain waters away from the building."

Alec nodded. "But?"

"They were first found in Egyptian and Chinese construction, long before the French or Spanish came to be," Jacques said. Alec didn't like where this was going. At all. The mere mention of Egyptian and Chinese histories put him on edge. "They always resembled the shape of an animal. A lion-like wolf or dragon-like creature."

Everyone was now standing in the room listening.

Jacques continued. "There is a French legend dating back to the seventh century where a chancellor of the king tells how he saved the people of Rouen from a monster called Gargouille. La Gargouille was said to have been the typical dragon-type creature with bat-like wings, a long neck, and the ability to breathe fire from its mouth."

"Willem said they breathed fire," Alec whispered. "Like a dragon."

Jacques nodded. "The legend states that the creature cannot be killed with fire. That is why the heads are mounted and water courses through their throats, so they cannot breathe fire."

"They were turned to stone," Eiji said softly.

Alec nodded. "What else?"

"The most famous are those at Notre Dame, but they are found the world over, Alec," he said. "There isn't a continent that doesn't have them."

Oh, fuck.

"The Tower Bridge in London; Milan, Italy; Wat Pho in Thailand; Angkor Wat in Cambodia; Candi Kalasan Temple in Indonesia; Chavin gargoyles of Chaupimarca, Peru; Valencia, Spain."

Alec put his hand up to stop him. "I get the idea. They're everywhere."

Jacques gave a nod. "They are."

Alec didn't need to remind anyone that humans warped actual history to protect themselves.

"So, these lycan-type creatures have been turned into gargoyles?" Kole asked. "Those statues on church walls always gave me the creeps."

Alec nodded. "I agree."

"Lycan, dragon, chimera," Jodis said. "What exactly are they?"

"Zoan," Alec reminded them.

Alec saw a reel of images flash through Cronin's mind. He was picturing the gargoyles he'd seen. They were a mix of sharp teeth, grotesque faces, sharp claws, some with wings, and some without. Then he pictured the Zoan Alec had shown him in his mind. They were distinctly similar. Then he studied the memory of the Zoan, searching for something. "Alec, do you recall seeing wings? Some gargoyles have wings."

"They wore cloaks and hoods. I couldn't see them clearly," he said, examining the memory again and sharing it with Cronin so he could see with him. "I'd rather they didn't have wings, you know, because seriously, I don't need them to be able to fly as well."

"It would explain the myth of dragons," Eiji said. "They are a symbol of my Japanese culture, but I have never seen or heard of anything outside of fables."

"Even fables have to come from somewhere," Eleanor said.

"Eleanor, can you see *anything* to do with the Zoan?" Cronin asked.

She shook her head. "No. Alec, if you cannot—outside of what they decide to show you—then I certainly cannot."

Alec nodded. He could see everything Eleanor saw, and like him and Jorge, she saw nothing. "So, to kill them, I need to turn them to stone?" Alec asked. "Which'd be easy enough if I had my powers when I see them, but I don't."

"Can you level the playing field?" Jodis asked.

"How?" Cronin countered.

Alec saw where her train of thought had gone. "Jodis wonders if I can manipulate time like they do. If it's a talent I don't know I have." He shook his head. "If I can, I have no way of knowing how to."

"Can you bring them here?" Eiji asked. "When they reveal themselves to you, can you somehow bring them to this reality?"

"How can I when I have no powers against them?" Alec repeated.

"I wonder if they have an inhibitor." Jodis pressed. "Meaning, I wonder if one of them has the power to block yours."

"I don't know!" Alec cried. "I have no powers against them! I can't see or hear or feel anything from them!"

Everyone took a step back, and Alec realized his frustration had billowed out from him. "Okay, he's had enough,"

Cronin said quietly. He put a protective hand on Alec's back.

Alec sighed loudly and dropped his head, immediately feeling bad for not having better control of his emotions. He reeled them in and turned in Cronin's arms to face him. "No, they're right. We need to talk this out." He fisted the shirt at Cronin's waist and pulled him against him, instantly feeling calmer. He closed his eyes and rested his forehead on Cronin's cheek, reveling in the peace he felt from him. "I won't know what I can do against these Zoan until I see them again. But maybe we should start with the portal they came through. Willem mentioned the Göbekli Tepe."

"Yes, we should," Jodis said.

"What's one more country?" Alec deadpanned and leapt them to the vast desert plains of Turkey.

GÖBEKLI TEPE WAS one of the oldest known archeological finds in history, dating some six thousand years *before* the Egyptian pyramids. It was a series of circular pits cut into the eroded dirt hill, and even though it was classified as a stone circle, to Alec it looked more like a group of holes in the ground than it did a stone circle. It was nothing like Callanais or Stonehenge. Known as a *temenos*, the main pit was a dug out circular hole in the plateau lined with standing stones. Where the likes of Stonehenge were huge megaliths standing above the ground, these standing stones were in the hollowed out circle. Filled in and buried around ten thousand years ago, but subsequently excavated by erosion and time, and more recently, by man.

Alec couldn't help but wonder if they'd been buried ten thousand years ago for a very good reason.

The nine stones, intermittently spaced in the main pit, lined the walls where they'd been dug out. Each one was twenty feet high but standing in a deliberate formation. Whomever, or whatever, had put them there, did so with great purpose. And given their age and the tools and skill available in that era, they did so very well.

Archeologists were right to assume it was one of the most critical finds in anthropology. These stones were *old*. They were the oldest known artifacts, not just in the study of henges and stone monuments, but in human history.

If it were humans that created them, that is. And Alec didn't think it was.

Each stone must have weighed twenty tons, and the only living creatures able to maneuver such a thing into a pit couldn't have been human. Each pillar was carved with animal engravings: depictions of dog-like and lizard-like creatures.

Zoan.

Creatures that resembled wolves and dragons etched into these stones could not have been a coincidence.

Alec ran his fingers along the cold etchings in the first stone, feeling the rough and crumbling texture of the limestone. "If the portal opened here, would it be right to assume this is where it has to be reopened?"

Cronin shot him a look. "Reopened?"

"For them to leave," Alec explained. "If this is the door they came through, then would they not leave the same way?"

Cronin looked thoughtful. "Possibly. Or we can just kill them."

Alec shrugged. "It would be helpful if we knew how."

"True." Cronin jumped down into the pit and inspected another stone. "Can you see or feel anything here?"

Alec closed his eyes and kept his hand on the stone. He took a deep breath and searched the vast expanse of his mind. "Nothing. Not even a hum of energy."

Jodis inspected a stone at the mouth of the pit. "From the research I could find, this pit was filled in in the Stone Age."

"For good reason, I'd imagine," Alec repeated his own thought from earlier. "Whoever filled it in ten thousand years ago, must not have wanted a repeat performance of whatever came out of it."

Eiji nodded. "It is eerie, no?"

Cronin agreed. "Yes. Göbekli Tepe translated means potbelly hill, so I can only assume those who named it believed the creatures lived in and escaped from the belly of the mountain."

"I'm half tempted to send a quake through this place," Alec said lowly. "To make sure nothing else comes out of it. But I can't if we need to send them back through here."

Then Alec glanced at Eiji, something Cronin didn't miss. "What was that?" Cronin asked him. "He thought something that surprised you."

Alec nodded. "Tell them, Eiji."

"It was just an errant thought," Eiji said. "This is a hill or a mound, yes? I couldn't help but wonder if, ten thousand years ago when it was built, if it was a pyramid."

Cronin stared at him, then at Alec and Jodis too. "There are no bodies buried here. It's a portal, is it not?"

"Well yes," Jodis agreed. "But you recall when we fought Keket and we searched under the Sphinx for the body of Ra, there was a circular room with stone pillars. They even call it the Egyptian Circular Temple."

"And under Mount Li where we met Genghis Khan," Eiji added. "What was he standing on?"

"A stone platform," Cronin answered. "A *circular* stone platform."

"What do the stone circles mean?" Alec asked. "I became a vampire in a stone circle. It gave the energy needed, the power, along with the elements of wood, fire, water, metal, the sun, and the moon. All of those things combined is what it took for me to change."

"Wait," Cronin said. "How many other circle pits are believed to be at this site?"

"Nine," Jodis said. "There are nine smaller circular pits."

Cronin smiled. "An orthocentric system."

"A what?" Alec blinked. He could see a network of geometry in Cronin's mind, a triangle and nine circles, all turning within each other, sliding and rotating, yet keeping the same space. "What the hell is that? I might have an untold depth of knowledge and use of many languages, but even so, I cannot speak Pythagorian."

Jodis smiled at him. "A nine-point circle can be constructed for any given triangle. It is named so because it passes through nine significant concyclic points defined from the triangle: the foot of each altitude, the midpoint of each side of the triangle, and the midpoint of the line segment from each vertex of the triangle to the orthocenter."

Alec blinked again. He could see the diagrams in his mind, the mathematical equations that directed the conclusions, but what it meant to him, he had no clue. "Yep, still got nothing."

Jodis tried again. "The theory is that the circle which passes through the feet of the altitudes of a triangle is tangent to all four circles, which in turn are tangent to the three sides of the triangle, giving nine points."

Alec stared at her, then looked at Eiji and Cronin. "Okay, Jodis is speaking in tongues."

Eiji laughed, but Cronin simplified the nine point circle thing. *Thank God.* "Each circle circumference has nine points which, given geometrical and mathematical methods, form a triangle."

"Okaaaaay," Alec said cautiously.

"The nine points in the circumference are not equal, like a pizza," Eiji said with a smile. "Imagine a pizza cut with uneven slices."

Alec nodded. *That* he understood. "Nine-point circles with pepperoni, that I understand."

Eiji and Cronin laughed, and even Alec laughed at his own joke. Jodis sighed at them, but turned around and looked at the nine standing stones in the main pit. "There are nine. I am certain if we could see a bird's eye view of this area, each stone would mark one of the nine points that made the pyramidal mound we're standing on."

Cronin nodded. "It's very interesting."

"Yes," Alec cried. "But what does it mean?"

"The source of power is what opened the portal, Alec," Cronin said. "The geometrical studies of how a nine-point circle related to a triangle was only discovered by mankind in the nineteenth century. This"—he waved his hand around the dirt pit—"was built using that exact theorem over ten thousand years ago."

Alec took a deep breath as he realized what this meant. "So, twelve thousand years ago, someone or some*thing*, was building a geometrical energy source to create portals for strange creatures to use?"

Cronin gave a hard nod. "Yes."

Alec ran his hand through his hair. "Willem said these Zoan creatures must be old for them to use the oldest portal.

But twelve thousand years.... How the hell can we beat something that has ten millennia of intelligence on us?"

No one answered.

Alec sighed. "All geometry and talk of energy sources to open portals aside," he said, "the bottom line is, if they've been killed before, we can kill them again. We need to find out how."

Eiji clapped his hands together and did a weird kind of dance. "Yes! And we have ourselves another mystery to solve."

"Settle down Scooby Doo," Alec deadpanned. "This one kinda feels bigger than the others."

Alec could see in Eiji's mind that he had no idea who Scooby Doo was, but he still smiled. "I seem to recall you saying the same thing last time."

Cronin firmly put both arms around Alec and a growly-purr rumbled in his chest. "If no one objects, I'd like some more time alone with Alec."

Of course no one did, though Eiji rolled his eyes.

"Alec, can you leap them back to New York?" Cronin asked.

"Of course."

Alec saw flashes of Cronin's intentions in his mind, and with a chuckle, he waggled his eyebrows to Eiji, and they disappeared.

ALEC FOUND himself on his back in a strange, plush hotel bed with Cronin lying over him, nestled between his legs. It was an executive suite of some fancy hotel that wasn't in use. The doors were locked; the voices he heard beyond them were speaking Italian. "Venice?"

Cronin smiled down at him. "It is a beautiful city."

"Don't you think we should be back in New York, helping with research or something?"

Cronin shook his head slowly and pushed Alec's hair from his forehead. "The talk of wars reminds me of what is important. And that is you. It might be selfish and unfair to the others, but I want time with you, *fear-cèile*."

My husband.

"I love it when you call me that," Alec whispered, his heart too big for his chest. "M'cridhe."

"My husband, my heart," Cronin repeated, the words barely a murmur. He leaned down and kissed Alec then. His hands cradled Alec's face and he moaned into his mouth.

Not breaking the kiss, Alec wrapped his arms around him and opened his legs wider. Still fully clothed, they held each other tight and made out like desperate teenagers.

Using his empathic powers, Alec expanded the love and desire he felt into Cronin. Cronin broke the kiss to gasp back a breath, and Alec traced his fingertips along his cheek. "That is how much I love you."

Cronin's whole body writhed as Alec's words sank through to his bones, and when he looked back down at Alec, his eyes were blackened pools of desire. "Can I have you?" Cronin asked huskily. "I want to be inside you."

Using his ability to leap objects or people to him, in his mind he sought out the half bottle of lube from their bedside drawer and made it appear on the bed beside them.

Cronin smiled, showing his fangs, which sent a jolt of desire straight to Alec's cock. "I want you inside me." Alec breathed the words. "Your cock in my ass. Your teeth in my neck."

Cronin's eyes bloomed with want, and he kissed Alec

harder this time. They were careful with their clothes; things tended to rip to ribbons when Alec didn't concentrate on his new vampire strength. When they were finally naked, Alec lay back on the bed, spread his legs, and slowly stroked his cock.

Cronin's nostrils flared.

I want you, Cronin. Alec's words wisped through Cronin's mind like sensual smoke. *Remind me that I am yours.*

Cronin crawled over the bed to be between Alec's legs. He smeared lube over his cock and over Alec's entrance and aligned himself. He leaned over Alec so he could kiss him, and Alec gripped his face so he could see it in Cronin's eyes as he pushed into him.

He saw every flicker of emotion in Cronin's eyes and in his mind. The sensations were so intense and pure. Alec felt every sensation, every emotion, two-fold—both Cronin's and his own—and he fed it to Cronin so he could feel it too.

It was so intoxicating. It was ten times better than the sex they'd had when Alec was human, a pleasure Alec couldn't have even dreamed of. But it was different now. They were so in tune with each other, made for each other.

Alec cupped Cronin's face as Cronin thrust in and out of him, their eyes never closing, never blinking until Alec craned his neck in invitation. Cronin licked Alec's throat before he scraped his fangs over the skin.

"Cronin, please." Alec moaned. He wanted to be impaled at both ends, to be owned, without doubt. He wanted to give himself completely. And the way Cronin held him and pushed into him, it was like he was trying to crawl inside him, trying to become one with him.

Cronin sank his teeth into Alec's neck as he came deep

inside him. Cronin's pleasure induced Alec's response and he followed at the same time.

Cronin licked the punctured skin on Alec's neck and kissed up his jaw. He put his hands to either side of Alec's face, pushing his hair off his forehead and softly kissed him as they simmered down.

Eventually Alec rolled them over so Cronin was on his back, and he cleaned them up a little. He kissed his chin, the hollow at his throat, and finally the silver scar on his chest. "Thank you," Alec whispered. "For knowing what I need."

"My intentions are not completely pure," Cronin said with a smirk. "My own needs were also a contributing factor."

Alec snorted out a laugh. "Well, your *contributing factors* were well received."

Cronin chuckled and let his arms sprawl out over the bed, quite content, it seemed, to let Alec do what he wanted with him. He had a sated, glazed look to his eyes and a lazy smirk. "You are so fucking sexy," Alec murmured. He kissed the scar on Cronin's chest one more time before finding his mouth again, kissing him deeply.

Cronin wrapped his arms around Alec's shoulders and hooked his legs around Alec's thighs. Cronin's kiss was hard and deep. His hips rose off the bed, begging with his body to be had for the taking. Alec obliged eagerly, slicking Cronin with lube and then his own cock, and he pushed into Cronin in one long thrust.

This time when they made love, they held hands and kissed softly. Quiet gasps and long moans filled the room as Alec radiated the love he felt so Cronin could never doubt exactly how he felt. Cronin's eyes closed tight, his jaw slack, his head pushed back, and his neck corded as Alec came inside him.

And for a perfect moment, their minds, souls, and bodies became one.

Cronin clung to Alec, tightening his hold. "I wish we could stay this way forever. I wish I could keep you here, safe."

"I wish that too," Alec said, peppering kisses down Cronin's jaw and sucking on his earlobe.

A shiver ran through Cronin's body, and he chuckled. "Do you think the others would miss us for a few centuries?"

Alec pulled back so he could see Cronin's face. He ran his hand through his ginger hair. "We can't expect others to fight for us."

"I know. I just wish it weren't so."

"Me too." Alec slowly pulled out of Cronin and rolled so they were on their sides, completely wrapped in each other's arms. "Though we could rest here a short while before we go back, yes?"

Cronin answered with a sleepy purr.

CRONIN WAS reluctant to return to New York. He knew they must, and he knew they'd been gone too long as it was, but he still would have rather taken Alec to some obscure, secret place where no one could find him.

Though with The Zoan—who, it seemed, tracked him in his mind—hiding was futile. It didn't matter where he was or what he was doing. If they wanted him to see something, they simply did exactly that.

But Alec was keen to get back and start piecing together the puzzle that he'd been once again thrown into.

"Nice of you to join us," Eiji joked. "Though I'm grateful you left to—" He sniffed Alec and scrunched up his nose. "—do whatever it is you did."

Alec laughed loudly. "We showered and everything!"

Alec and Eiji had become close friends, and this pleased Cronin greatly. They were, as the saying went, like peas in a pod. They had similar senses of humor and Cronin would often find them together, laughing about something—usually something crude or childish.

"Quit your whining," Alec said with another laugh. "Or I'll give you a complete mental replay."

Eiji paled and his hands dropped to his sides. "Please don't ever do that."

Alec clapped him on the shoulder and turned to face everyone in the living room. They each sat with books or a laptop, making notes and cross referencing. There had been great progress, and Jodis had put most of them in chronological order.

"The first, and perhaps the most alarming, is the *Epic of Gilgamesh* scripts. In approximately 2100 BC, there was a creature known as Humbaba, which is described as a wolf-like man with a body of thorny scales." Jodis looked at Alec. "It also breathed fire."

"Oh, crap," Alec mumbled.

"That's not all," Jodis said. "The original stone tablet these scripts were carved upon bore the words *Sha naqba īmuru*, which, from ancient Mesopotamian times, roughly translates to 'it begins with he who sees the unknown.'"

"Sees the unknown?" Cronin repeated. "Like Alec sees the Zoan?"

Jodis gave a nod. "I believe so. These scripts were either

made by someone who knew of the visions or by someone who saw them firsthand, like Alec sees them."

Alec leaned against the dining table and folded his arms. He looked at Cronin for a moment, seemingly not sure what to say. He swallowed hard, then turned back to Jodis. "What else?"

"The well-known story of Saint George bears some credence," she replied. "In the second century BC, it is said he slayed a fire breathing dragon. Whether it is fact or fiction is still debated to this day, but given that the story remains the same in many different cultures and religions, I'd believe it to be closer to truth than not."

Alec closed his eyes and rubbed his temples. "And?"

"There are recorded Ukrainian histories dated to the sixth century that claim an entire race of people—the Neuri —to be werewolves," Jodis said. "Though I think we can forgive the term werewolf. Locals of that time would have likened them to wolves, being the most feared wild animal in those areas, not knowing the difference between wolves and lycan."

"I think we can forgive much of the human histories for this confusion," Jacques added. "It wasn't until the sixteenth century that a scientific difference was clarified."

"There were a lot of witch hunts throughout Europe through medieval times, as we know," Jodis gave Cronin a dark look. "Though many creatures are listed as werewolves, the true nature of these creatures may not ever be known."

"The first instance of the word werewolf, be it an actual werewolf or a lycan, was in the eleventh century," Jacques said. "Though the first lycan story was told in Greek mythology." He read from an old text. "'A doctor, Marcellus of Sides, in the second century documented lycanthropy was a form of depression and prescribed bloodletting.'"

"Oh, excellent," Alec said sarcastically. "That would have ended well for a blood drinking animal."

Jacques continued. "'In the seventh century, an Alexandrian physician by the name of Aegineta wrote of humans who became wolves and howled in the cemeteries, killing people. Also prescribed bloodletting.'"

"Then with the introduction of Christianity throughout Europe, these stories of lycans and other shape-shifting creatures were put to an end with witch hunts and religious persecution of demons and Satanists. No one even dared write about them for fear of retribution." Jodis closed the book in front of her. "Though there was a doctor by the name of Weyers who wrote about demonism, including lycanthropy, in the sixteenth century. Needless to say, he wasn't very popular."

Jodis went on to add, "So for a few hundred years, such creatures only survived in folklore and pagan tales spoken around campfires instead of written down. Then we find medical cases from the sixteenth century, most citing madness and clinical lycanthropy."

"And outside of Europe?" Alec asked.

"Asian dragon myths stem from the beginning of time to this very day," Eiji said. "In most countries, religions, and art."

"There's a dragon in the Old Testament," Kole said. "A seraph serpent. A fiery reptile. Could it have been a fire-breathing lizard with wings... a dragon... type thing?" He shook his head like he couldn't believe he was saying such things.

Alec snorted. "Weird, huh?"

Kole looked so much like his son when he smiled. "Just a little."

"There is an African people," Eleanor said, "the Nyoro tribes, who believe in ancient times that the first humans were chameleons."

"A lizard that changes color?" Cronin asked.

"Or shape," Alec added.

"Could it be that the Zoan present themselves in the form most horrific to the human culture it faces?" Eiji asked rhetorically. It was an interesting notion, and quite possible, Cronin agreed. Eiji went on. "Throughout Europe, the wolf was most feared, so that is what they saw. Throughout Asia, it was the evil dragons."

"And what do I see?" Alec asked.

"Their truest form. You see under their human façade to the beast underneath," Jodis said. She looked around at everyone. "We've all seen what Alec has seen. Wild teeth, scaly skin. Could it not be a hybrid of lycan and dragon?"

Alec turned to Jacques. "Tell the others what you just thought," he said to him. "Sorry for hearing that, but it's a valid point."

"Oh," Jacques said, blushing a little. "I don't know what made me think of it, but getting back to the gargoyles... there was a remarkable case in France in 1450 called the Paris Wolves. A pack of forty or more 'wolf-men' reportedly killed a hundred people. The pack was eventually lured and cornered, and they were killed."

"Tell them where," Alec pressed.

"At the doors of the Notre Dame Cathedral."

Cronin knew why Alec thought this was important. He stared at Jacques. "When were the gargoyles added to Notre Dame?"

"There have been many additions to the gargoyles that grace the exterior walls," Jacques explained.

"When were the first ones added?" Cronin pressed.

"In 1450."

Jodis smiled. "It cannot be a coincidence. They are one and the same."

Cronin nodded. "It would appear so."

"The original gargoyles were removed and replaced in the nineteenth century," Jacques said. "There's a crypt beneath the cathedral. From what we learned in history, statues and such things are kept there."

Cronin, Alec, Jodis, and Eiji all smiled at one another. Then Alec clapped Eiji on the shoulder again and said, "Looks like we're going to France."

Then Cronin watched as Alec froze, for just the blink of an eye, his face neutral, his eyes glazed over. Alec sucked back a gasping breath and stumbled forward. Cronin leapt to catch him, and when he held him and helped him to his feet, he smelled it. The most delectable scent, an essence Cronin would kill for.

Alec's blood.

CHAPTER SEVEN

VAMPIRES HAD IMPECCABLE BALANCE, coupled with agility and speed, and a perfect sense of space and distance. Alec could balance on the edge of a dime if he needed to. So losing that equilibrium was disconcerting, to say the very least.

The sense of falling, of stumbling and losing his sense of awareness was the most unnerving.

"Alec!" Cronin's arms were around him, keeping him upright and safe.

Alec's reality came back to him like a vacuum, sucking back into current time and space, and he had full control of his body and mind, vampire talents included. He could hear and feel Cronin's anguish and the internal war to leap or stay.

"Stay," Alec whispered. He was breathless, which was disturbing in itself. He noticed everyone in the room was on their feet, watching on in horror. Except Eiji and Jodis. They had assumed a protective stance around him, crouched and ready to defend him. He felt their alarm, their worry. "I'm okay," he told them. "They're gone."

"You're bleeding!" Cronin's voice was strangled.

Alec looked down at his arm to see that he was, in fact, as Cronin had said, bleeding. He'd not felt it before Cronin had mentioned it. Then he remembered....

Cronin put his hands to Alec's face, scanning every inch of him for further injury. "Alec, m'cridhe, tell me what happened!"

"The Zoan," he replied in a whisper. He then whispered directly into Cronin's mind, *I need to sit down.* He swayed on his feet, then found himself on the sofa with Cronin kneeling in front of him.

Cronin made a pained whining sound, his hands touching Alec's face, his neck, his chest. "Please tell me you are well."

Alec nodded and gave him a weak smile. "I'm fine."

Jodis ripped Alec's bloodied shirtsleeve off at the shoulder. "The wound is deep but you're healing quickly enough."

Focus turned to the cut on his arm. Claw marks, each three-inches-long, were torn into the outside of his bicep. Jagged and deep, the three gashes had bled profusely, but were almost healed now, though Alec's arm was stained red down to his fingers.

Vampire blood was not appealing to other vampires in the way a human's was, except to their mate. And Alec could read and feel Cronin's discomfort—he was protective and territorial over Alec's blood, as all mates were, but fueled with his fear for Alec's safety. Alec knew Cronin was close to losing it. "I should wash my arm," he offered quietly.

Cronin's nostrils flared and he shook his head. "Don't move. I will do it." And with that, he disappeared.

Alec looked up at the others and saw Kole. His father looked pale and afraid. "Alec?" His voice was so unsure, his steps toward him shaky. His dad sat beside him and put his hand on Alec's leg. "You okay, son?"

Alec could see right into his dad's mind. He could see himself through his father's eyes, and it was a humbling sight. There he was, looking a little pale, bloodied, and his vampire fangs clearly visible. Yet, Kole still looked at him like he always had—like a father who simply loved his son. As much as Alec had changed, Kole's love for him remained the same. Alec's heart flooded with warmth and humility. Alec squeezed his father's hand. "I'm okay, Dad."

Cronin appeared in front of him again, holding a bowl of warm water and a cloth. The water swooshed in the bowl from leaping, yet Cronin remained perfectly still. He knelt before him and gently took Alec's hand. And with the dampened cloth, he washed Alec's arm. With slow, precise, reverent strokes, Cronin cleaned him. There was so much love in each movement, it stole Alec's breath.

Eiji's eyes were hard and serious. "Alec, how do you feel?"

Alec thought for a moment. Physically he was fine, a little shaken up, cut, but almost fully healed. But then he remembered everyone's concern and fear for him, how Eiji and Jodis moved to defend and protect him, how his father saw him, how Cronin tended to him. "I feel very humbled, to be honest."

Cronin's gaze shot to his. "Alec?"

"Everyone's fussing over me," Alec said, embarrassed. "I'm okay, really."

"You're not okay," Cronin said, his voice a low growl. "They hurt you, Alec! You are not okay. This is *not* okay."

Alec put his hand to Cronin's face and stared intently into his eyes. "Cronin, m'cridhe. I'm okay."

"Alec," Eiji interrupted. He was rarely so concerned, and his serious manner now had everyone's attention. "Did they cut you with a blade or was it a claw? A tooth? Can you remember what they injured you with? It looks like a claw...."

"I can show you if you like?" Alec said. He scanned the faces looking back at him. "I can show all of you."

A show of nods went around the room, so Alec recalled the moment this latest encounter started and pushed the memory into the minds of those around him.

One second Alec was joking and excited about going to Paris, the next his whole vision changed. Like time stood still, everyone in the room was frozen except Alec and five Zoan creatures, who now stood in front of him. Cloaked again in heavy dark robes, they stood in an arrow formation: the leader, Alec assumed, at the speared front. Alec could see their grotesque muzzles flickering in and out of view under their human skins.

"Your studies of us are intriguing," the leader said. Its voice was raspy and deep. "Though you only need to have asked, Ailig, and we would have told you."

Again Alec tried to unleash his powers, sending a rush of crippling pain toward them. But nothing. He tried to see in their minds, to freeze them, set them on fire, make them explode, change color, anything. And again, nothing worked.

"What do you want?" Alec finally asked.

"You sent for us," the leader said with a sneer. "An equal reaction to your birth to this life."

"Why now?" Alec asked. "It's been a year."

"Time is of no matter to us," the leader said. "A concept

made by mankind to gauge no more than the passing of their unimportant lives."

"What do you want?" Alec repeated.

"Power absolute," the leader said with a menacing smile. Then Alec was bombarded with mental images of Zoans feeding on the hearts of humans in the streets of New York. It was a bloodied, horrific carnage. "Your offense is hypocritical," the leader said. "We are no different than you."

Alec shook his head to clear the images of the massacre of the human race. "Is that why I am your enemy?"

"You are the key, are you not?"

"I am."

"The key with which our world was locked."

"I don't understand," Alec said. "Locked what? How could I do anything when I have no powers against you?"

The leader laughed, a spine-chilling sound that morphed from a sinister laugh to an angry roar. "You are the reason we are here."

"Then why am I your enemy?" Alec asked them. Then answering his own question, he realized why. To declare one as an enemy means to fear them. And if it was Alec who opened the portal to their world and they feared him, then that could only mean one thing. "Because I can close the portal. I can send you back."

The leader gnashed his teeth and stepped in closer to him. "Look around you, Ailig. You are without power here."

"Yet I am still not alone," Alec replied. He had no idea why or where those words came from, but he knew them to be true.

Alec tried again to breach their minds but could feel nothing. He tried to find a weakness in their defenses, searching with the expanses of his mind, but there was nothing. So, he did the only thing he could think of.

Alec lunged at the leader, needing to see if he could physically touch him. If he held no mental power in this realm, then maybe he had some physical capabilities.

The leader snarled and raised his hand—his large claws like razors—and swiped at Alec. It was just the barest tips of the talons that grazed Alec's arm.

Alec felt everything at once, and the Zoan's reaction was immediate.

Collectively they all gasped, the leader howled in some kind of pain, and they vanished. The room, the sights, and sounds sucked back into place, and Alec, still lunging forward, fell into Cronin's arms.

NO ONE MOVED, no one spoke for a long moment as they processed what Alec had just shown them. Cronin was the first to move. He threw his arms around Alec and held him so tight. "He could have killed you."

Jodis nodded toward Alec's almost healed arm. "That was the claws that ripped through you, Alec."

"It's what concerned me, brother," Eiji said to Alec. "Is there fact in the folklore that to be cut open by tooth or talon will turn you into what they are?" Everyone watched Eiji. Alec had never seen him so worried. "Can a lycan change a human into a lycan if they bite or claw their victim? As vampires we bite to change, yes? Are they not the same laws?"

Cronin growled, low and warning, and his fangs were bared. Not at Eiji but at what he was implying.

"This is why I asked how you were feeling, Alec?" Eiji said, concern etched in his eyes and his mind. *Please tell me you are well, brother.*

"I feel fine. I feel... normal. All vampire," Alec said, as

calmly and as reassuringly as he could. He looked down at his arm. The bleeding gashes were gone, closed over, sealed with angry red lines. "I'm almost fully healed."

"There are no ill-effects?" Jodis asked.

Alec shook his head. "No. None. Maybe the myth is wrong. Maybe lycan are born, not changed? Maybe vampires can't be changed from their vampire state. Maybe it's just me, and I can't be changed to lycan, the same way I couldn't be changed into a vampire, you know, before I changed into a vampire."

No one found his attempt at humor funny. Not even Eiji.

"Well, there was something about your blood they didn't like," Eleanor said.

"They didn't like it," Jodis said. "Whether they were alarmed that you touched him, Alec, or because of your blood, I can't be certain."

Alec was pretty sure it wasn't the physical contact. "When he cut me, in that moment, I could feel and hear like I can now. You felt that change? In my memory?"

Jodis nodded.

"What did it taste like?" Alec asked them.

"Metal," Jacques answered. "Metallic."

"Mercury," Cronin said. "They tasted mercury."

Alec looked at him and smiled. "Can't be a coincidence, can it?"

He shook his head slowly. "I wouldn't believe so."

"But Cronin," Jodis countered, "you cannot taste it when you drink from Alec."

"No," he agreed. "I can't. But they did."

"What is the significance of mercury?" Kole asked. "From when Alec was changed?"

Cronin nodded. "Yes." How Alec was changed, with

the silver rivers of mercury in the underground pits of China being a critical component in the process, was now common knowledge in the vampire communities around the world. With the four elements—Alec being the fifth—both the sun and the moon in the sky at the same time and the circle of stones becoming a circle of light, and how Cronin had used his temporary powers to transfer the power of life into Alec, it was certainly not a typical transformation.

Needless to say, word had spread quickly that the vampire key had been born to save them.

They were just blissfully ignorant at the time that these events had triggered a portal opening so Hell itself could slither through.

Jodis smiled at Alec. "Whatever the reason, I think we've found the Zoan's Achilles' heel."

"Their Achilles' heel maybe," Cronin countered, "though they still hold the advantage; we cannot see them. They do not exist in our world, or time, or whatever or wherever it is. Only Alec can see them, and without his powers, he cannot fight them."

Everyone was quiet, and what glimmer of hope might have sparked, slowly faded away.

"Alec," Jacques said, breaking the silence. "When you were talking with them, you realized they'd declared themselves your enemy because it is you that will defeat them."

Alec nodded. "Yes, it makes sense."

"Agreed. But they recoiled from your blood *after* that," Jacques offered. "They feared defeat from you *before* they knew your blood smelled of mercury."

"So they know there's another way you can kill them," Eiji finished for him. "We just need to figure out what that is."

"We need answers," Cronin said.

"First, we need to hold that council meeting," Jodis said, "with all elders, the world over. The Zoan have made a threat to all vampires, and the elders should be told, and maybe they know something that will help us. Lore long disregarded, anything."

"I agree," Alec said. "They should be prepared. Though I'd prefer a video conference so we speak to everyone at the same time. Can we do that?"

Jodis nodded. "Of course. I'll start making calls."

"Good," Alec said. "And a coven meeting. Not just for the elders, but we should hold an East Coast coven meeting as well. The vision I saw was carnage on the streets of New York City, and they should know what I saw too."

"If we give the Eastern coven two days to gather," Eiji said, "that will give us some time to find out what we can."

Then Cronin said, "And if we can't ask the living Zoan, then we shall see what the dead ones can tell us. We should go look at some gargoyles."

"Paris?" Alec asked.

Cronin gave a nod. "And London."

Alec gave him a smile. "We better let Kennard know we're coming."

Cronin stared into his eyes. *Alec, forgive my selfishness, but before we go, may I have a moment alone with you?*

"Of course," he said. Then Alec announced to the room, "I need a minute or two with Cronin before we leave. We won't be long."

Jodis already had the phone to her ear, and Eiji was making mental jokes at Cronin for only taking *a minute or two*. Alec rolled his eyes. He pictured the most perfect place on earth and leapt Cronin there.

THE SMILE CRONIN gave Alec when he saw where he was, was wide and warm yet tinged with worry.

A soft breeze gently caressed the long grass of the old battlefield, and they stood facing each other in the moonlight. "What is it, Cronin?" Alec asked.

"Can I show you something?" Cronin asked. "A memory."

"Of course."

"It is from my human days," he whispered, his eyes downcast. "I have very few memories from that time, but this... well, this I remember."

"Cronin?"

Without speaking another word, Cronin put his hands up, palms forward. Alec put his palms to Cronin's, and he opened his mind.

Alec could hear an ancient melody, a Scottish song. Cronin was remembering the music from his human years, and flickers of a village wedding accompanied the memory. It was evening, there were people at tables, eating and drinking, a fire for warmth. A man's voice sang lilting words in Gaelic, of love and life, as the human Cronin watched the couple dance. They moved around each other in circles with only their foreheads and palms touching, their heels kicking up and toes pointed. Alec had seen traditional Scottish dances but never like this. Never anything so intimate.

But it wasn't just the dancing. Alec could feel the sense of longing Cronin felt while he watched them. As a human, he wanted to know what such love felt like. He wanted someone to dance with him like they danced. And a resigning ache burned in his chest, knowing the relationship he yearned for was not allowed. Not in those days. A man couldn't love another man. There would be no one to hold him, to look at him like that.

But now there was.

Oh, Cronin....

Alec took the song from Cronin's mind and played it back to him, and Alec started to move to the music. He mimicked the dance he saw in Cronin's memory, and Cronin's eyes closed slowly.

With their palms still touching, Alec moved right, Cronin moved left, so they were an arm width apart, and they turned in a circle. Then dropping their hands, Cronin slowly circled Alec, close but not touching. Alec could feel his presence, his heat, as he moved around him. And when Cronin was facing him again, they resumed their position but circled in the other direction. Their foreheads and palms touching, Alec could feel the swell of love and gratitude in Cronin's chest. A love so overwhelming and all-encompassing, it stole Alec's breath. Cronin closed his eyes but couldn't stop the tear that ran a solitary line down his cheek. Alec tilted Cronin's face upward and kissed him softly.

Cronin slowly opened his eyes. "Thank you, m'cridhe."

"Oh, Cronin, my heart." Alec pulled Cronin against him and held him close. Still moving his feet, they danced a slow, slow circle with Cronin's face buried in Alec's neck. The Scottish music still playing softly in their minds, and Cronin started to cry.

Cronin didn't need to speak. Alec could feel his sorrow, his fear, and a flurry of words swam through his mind. He was afraid; Cronin was afraid this enemy was too strong. He feared their days were numbered. He wondered how on earth an immortal was supposed to deal with death, and he wondered if Alec died, would his own death be simultaneous. He hoped it would be.

Alec stopped moving and cupped Cronin's face in both hands. "No." He shook his head. "No."

"They hurt you!" Cronin said as his eyes welled with fresh tears.

Alec looked down at his arm where the gashes had been but had since healed. "Cronin, my love, I'm fine."

"They hurt you!" he said again. "So it was just claws this time. Next time it could be a stake to the heart. We have no way to stop them, and if you were powerless against them, what hope do we have?"

Alec had never seen him so unsure, so afraid of anything! "Don't be afraid."

"We were supposed to have forever," Cronin whispered.

"We will."

Cronin shook his head. "You can't know that. You can't see it. How can we beat something we can't even see?"

"We will beat them," he said with more determination.

"I fear for your life. I fear you will feel pain, that they will do unspeakable things," Cronin shook his head before leaning into Alec's palm, and again he closed his eyes. "I fear for Jodis and Eiji. They are my family, and I worry for them. We were supposed to live forever. One year, Alec. I've had you for one year. A mere blink in time. I want forever," he growled, angry now. "It may be selfish of me to ask for it, and for all I've done, maybe I don't deserve it. But I want forever with you, and I will kill anyone who tries to take that from me."

Alec swallowed the lump in his throat. "Shhh." He let the Scottish music play again in their heads. "Dance with your husband."

Cronin smiled despite his teary eyes. He held out his hands again to begin the dance and raised his chin. "It would be my honor," he said.

"As it is mine," Alec said.

And there in their private field at Dunadd, they danced.

CHAPTER EIGHT

"ALEC!" Kennard greeted him warmly with a kiss to both cheeks. They met in Kennard's apartment in London, which was a warehouse-style loft. It was exquisitely furnished, yet Alec never felt it was a home. Though Kennard somehow looked in place there—he was dressed in his usual black jeans, boots, and designer coat; his blond hair styled up perfectly; his pretty elvish face completed his just-stepped-off-the-catwalk look.

"I am loath to see you looking so happy," Kennard said with a sparkle in his eyes. "I was hoping you'd be swayed by a certain Englishman's charms, but alas, your heart is still fated to a Scot."

Alec laughed, knowing all too well that a fated heart could never change. Kennard grinned impishly, shook hands with Eiji and Jodis, saying a brief hello, but soon turned back to Alec. Cronin was quick to put himself between them. "Still flirting with my husband, I see," Cronin said, laying his Scottish accent on thick. He was in a much better frame of mind after their quick timeout in Dunadd. "You'd think you'd have learned by now.

Though granted, the Brits weren't known for their scholars."

Kennard laughed loudly. "Need I remind you of the Battle of Floddon?"

Cronin snorted out a laugh. "That was a fixed battle and you know it. It cost me forty gold pieces. But the Battle of Haddon Rig, now that was a fair fight."

Kennard's shoulders shook as he laughed. "Ah Alec, he's still a sore loser after all these years."

Alec looked between them both. He could see memories from long ago in both their minds: a small room with a low ceiling, a lit fire, and their clothes from the sixteenth century, exchanging purses of coins. "You took bets on human battles?"

Kennard waved his hand. "We didn't create the quibbles between our countries. We simply wagered on the outcome."

"You know," Alec said, slipping his hand into the back pocket of Cronin's jeans. "I am jealous of the history you share."

Cronin turned a little so he could rest his forehead on Alec's cheek. "We cannot change what has passed, m'cridhe."

Kennard looked at them longingly and sighed. He no longer smiled. "'Fly envious Time, till thou run out thy race.'"

Cronin looked up at him and frowned. "Quoting Milton? Such words from you can only mean melancholy."

Kennard faked a smile and Alec saw in his mind when he decided not to bother holding up the façade. He could also see the look of sadness on Kennard's face burned all the way to his chest. "Kennard?" Alec question.

"It's just been some weeks for reflection," Kennard said.

"Maybe after you've lived as many years as I, Alec, you'll understand." Then Kennard glanced at Cronin. "Or perhaps not."

Alec felt then, rather than saw it, that it wasn't sorrow Kennard felt but loneliness. *You are not alone,* he whispered directly into Kennard's mind. Alec showed him mental images of all the English coven Alec had met, who each idolized Kennard and of course, Cronin, Eiji, and Jodis.

The difference between being alone and being lonely is an immeasurable void, Alec, Kennard replied. It was quickly followed by a pang of regret for acknowledging his emotions and even a dash of fear for showing a weakness.

Have you not ever asked a seer to look into your future? Alec asked him. *To see when your fated one comes along?*

No! He almost shouted the word in his head. Then he very reluctantly said, *What if they show me nothing? I think I'd rather not know.* He paused a moment and remembered Alec's words. *You said when?*

"Kennard," Alec said, letting go of Cronin and putting his hand on Kennard's arm instead. "When I was given these powers, I swore I wouldn't look into anyone's future. It's not fair or wise to meddle with things that cannot change. But if you want to know, I can show you something. But only if you want it. It's something you can't take back, so you need to be sure."

Kennard's eyes lit up despite his sullen mood. Alec could see his instant curiosity and excitement, but he caught himself before he spoke. "Does it breach some code of ethics or rule you imposed on yourself, you know, to show me such things? If I were to say yes, that is. Which I'm not sure I am."

"I told Cronin," Eiji said. "I could see his heart would join another, but not who or when or where. He was in a similar mood to yours, Kennard, wondering if he was to walk this earth alone forever."

Kennard frowned and nodded.

"It was a long few hundred years to wait from Eiji telling me to the day I found Alec," Cronin said quietly. "Five hundred and eighty-three, to be exact."

"Did it make it easier?" Kennard asked quietly. "Or worse?"

"So much better," Cronin answered. "Just knowing was enough. It lifted a weight from my heart."

Kennard licked his lips and nodded quickly. Cronin's words were ones he clearly understood.

It's okay Kennard. It's not something you need to decide right now, Alec told him.

"I want to," he said. "Quick. Before I change my mind."

Alec could see Kennard was certain. There was no doubt in his mind at all. Despite the words he said, he truly wanted to know.

So Alec reached into his own mind, into the swirls and flickers that were of things yet to happen, until he found what he was after. Instead of showing Kennard images, he showed him emotional charges. He showed Kennard a portion of how he would feel the day he met his fated one.

Kennard was stunned. "Is that how it feels? Is that me?"

Alec nodded. "I can't show you when or where or even what he looks like. I can't ruin it all for you. But yes, that is you. And that is not even a quarter of what you will feel."

Kennard's eyes welled with tears. Happy, grateful tears. "Wow."

Alec could feel Kennard's heart had bloomed in his chest, just a fraction of what he would feel the day he met his fated one, but it warmed Kennard through. Alec pulled Kennard in for a hug, which surprised Kennard, but was welcome nonetheless. "See? The whole lovey-dovey stuff between fated couples that makes you wanna puke isn't so bad, is it?" Alec asked.

Kennard laughed and pulled back from Alec, basically handing him back to Cronin. "No, and I won't even mind too much if he's Scottish."

Cronin snorted at that. "God forbid."

Kennard shot Alec a look. "He's not though, is he? Scottish, I mean. He's English, yes?"

Alec laughed and shook his head. "I'm not saying!"

Jodis put her hand on Kennard's arm. "I don't need Alec's powers to see how happy this news makes you."

Kennard took a deep breath and let it out slowly. He was smiling now, though it was an at-peace smile. "Thank you, Alec. I was completely unaware of how much I needed to see that. Or feel it, rather. I didn't *see* anything." He purred at Alec. "If you'd like to show me a little glimpse of what he looks like, I wouldn't mind."

Alec shook his head. "No. You'll know him when you see him."

"Or perhaps when I will see him?" he pushed, his eyes wide and hopeful.

"Nope."

Kennard huffed, but his pout soon morphed into a smile. "I'm still grateful." He moved fluidly around his apartment to the living room, where he waved his hand at the plush leather sofas so Alec, Cronin, Eiji, and Jodis would join him. "Well, my mood is so much better. I haven't even been to my club in a month," Kennard told them. "I've been wallowing for weeks, until you called, Alec. You said you needed to talk about something important? I apologize for monopolizing your time in my self-pity."

"It's no problem, Kennard," Alec replied. "I just wish

you'd have called us. We could have come to visit. I could have kicked your ass in Grand Theft Auto until you felt better. I kick Eiji's ass all the time."

Eiji shrugged and Kennard chuckled quietly. "Thank you. I'll keep that in mind. But your matter of importance, Alec. Haven't happened across another ancient madman that needs slaying?"

Alec made a face. "Well, about that...."

Kennard's mouth fell open. "Seriously? Alec, what is it with you and weird?"

Alec sighed. "I'm actually considering contacting Merriam-Webster and Oxford and asking them to reevaluate their definition of weird, because it's just not cutting it anymore."

"What is it this time?" Kennard asked. "The Yersinians are dead, the last of the Illyrians were taken care of, all the Egyptian gods have been sent back to the afterlife, even the Terracotta Army went back to statues when we left Qin's tomb. I mean, who else is there? Did those clay soldiers start to move again?"

Alec smiled at him. "Well actually, these are lycan-type creatures who came through a portal that seem to have the ability to stop time."

Kennard blinked.

"Oh," Alec added. "And I'm the only one who can see them."

Kennard glanced at each of them in turn, and seeing the seriousness on their faces, he sighed loudly. "Really, Alec? You're just not happy unless you're the center of attention, are you?" Alec barked out a laugh, and Kennard shook his head. "Alright, alright. So how are we going to kill them?"

AFTER ALEC HAD EXPLAINED the whole story of the Zoan—complete with showing him the memories of each encounter—Kennard was a lot more serious.

As the elder of the London coven, he'd already called a council meeting, not only for England but for all of Great Britain. Telling Alec he'd even suffer through a meeting with the Scots and the Welsh. Hell, he'd even call the Irish just for him. Alec could see in Kennard's mind that while he took the piss out of the Scots and Irish, he would also defend them like family.

"There are some notable gargoyles around London," Cronin said. "I'd hoped we could check them out while we're here. With your permission, of course."

Covens were fiercely territorial, and although none of them would probably mind if non-London vampires, such as Alec, started poking around their city, Cronin was showing a mere common courtesy by asking.

"Permission?" Kennard repeated. "For you, my dear friends, I shall give you a grand and personal tour."

THE GARGOYLES that graced the Tower Bridge were simply stone carvings. Alec hadn't known what to expect, but it was obvious the grotesques were simply ornamental design features.

The gargoyles at Westminster Abbey were plenty in number, but once again, strictly man-made with the purpose of either diverting roof water, or to ward away evil spirits. Which was funny to Alec, considering five vampires were inspecting them.

Even with Alec's perfect vampire vision, the cover of night gave the carved stone features an even more disturbing look. The play of shadows distorted the already unnerving characteristics.

Leaping inside the cathedral, inspecting vaults and hidden basements was easy enough, but Alec wasn't convinced any of the statues were anything but man-made. They were remarkable and fascinating, but not what he was looking for.

Eiji and Jodis had gone to search one of the vaulted undercrofts of the Abbey for any kind of gargoyle that might be a clue, and Kennard had searched the bell tower, while Alec and Cronin searched the Abbey itself.

Bored with their lack of findings, Alec took Cronin's hand and led him, as regally as he possibly could, to sit in the Coronation Chair. "Your seat, my king."

Cronin laughed and the sound echoed fantastically throughout the high-ceilinged room. He held his arms out from his body with poise, gracefully turned, and sat, rather dramatically, on the chair.

Eiji and Jodis walked into the Abbey, and Alec extended his arm and bowed to them and announced, "I present to you the King of Scotland."

Cronin waved and raised his chin. He laid on a thick Scottish brogue. "Aye. Beat the heart of a king, only for the man at his side."

Eiji bowed down. "And the Oscar goes to...."

Kennard cleared his throat from the side of the Abbey. He walked in and gave a petulant sniff. "I'm sure the Queen of England would be impressed with that performance."

Cronin grinned at him. "And I shall decree, be it noted in script and stone, that all Scots are better in bed and battle than ye Englishmen."

Kennard scowled at him. "Of all the things this country's Queen would call sacrilege of you sitting in that chair

—not that you're a vampire, or gay, or even married to an American—is that you're a bloody Scot."

Alec laughed at them. "That's King of Scots, thank you very much."

Kennard rolled his eyes and chose to ignore them. "I found nothing. Not that I truly know what to look for. I've seen nothing of the like of what Alec has shown me from his memories."

"Nor us," Jodis said. "There's nothing here."

Cronin tapped the fragile wooden armrest. "Except this fabulous chair."

Alec snorted. "Think it would look good in our apartment?"

Kennard hissed. "You're not taking the Coronation Chair!"

Cronin laughed, stood up, and stepped down from the chair. "Where to next?"

"Canterbury Cathedral," Kennard said.

Cronin put his hand out. "Let's go then." Alec, Jodis, and Eiji put their hands atop of his.

"Wait!" Kennard cried. He darted up to the Coronation Chair and sat in it. "Just so the last one to sit in it was English."

Cronin laughed again, and when Kennard came back over and put his hand over the others, Cronin leapt them to another famous English church.

Canterbury Cathedral was huge. Another cathedral built in the eleventh century, Gothic style, and quite frankly, Alec found it daunting. They searched the outside first, inspecting the hundreds of gargoyles: some large, some tiny, none of them what they were after.

Inside, the nave was huge, spectacular, and nothing short of a masterpiece of its time, but it was also sparse and cold—not in temperature but in feeling. Alec stared at the choir screen in particular. "Why are churches so damn creepy?" he whispered.

Cronin took his hand. "To humble the sinners, maybe?"

"To remind the poor that there is untouchable wealth in organized religion, which they shall give to yet never receive, or receive an eternity in damnation," Kennard added. Then he shrugged. "Or maybe I'm cynical about such things."

"Maybe." Jodis snorted delicately. "We'll take the library and chapel houses to the north," she said, and she and Eiji disappeared.

"I'll take the south," Kennard said.

"That leaves the crypts and tombs to us," Cronin said.

"Oh, goodie," Alec moaned.

"How does it fare that you, of all vampires, are spooked by a building?" Cronin asked as they took the stairs down to the crypt.

"Maybe there's some truth in these places warding out evil." Alec said, looking around the crypt.

Cronin stopped and stared at him. "You are not evil."

Alec barked out a laugh that echoed sharply right back at him. "I'm not exactly what humans would call good, either, Cronin." He walked through the columns, lightly touching the stone pillars with his fingers. "You know, when I was little, I thought vampires lived in huge castles in Transylvania or somewhere, all made from stone." He looked up at the vaulted ceilings. "But I couldn't think of anything worse."

Cronin studied him curiously for a moment. "This is just a building, Alec. Rich in history, yes. A place of worship for some, but still just a building. When it was constructed, there was no such material as drywall."

Alec shrugged it off and gave Cronin a smile. "I know. It's still creepy, though."

Cronin held out his hand. "Come on. There's nothing down here."

They walked back up the steps to the presbytery where they waited for the others. Alec could hear their thoughts as they searched the walls, ceilings, and the hidden compartments for any sign of the Zoan, gargoyles, lycan, or anything.

"They found nothing," Alec whispered.

Cronin sat in the Archbishop's throne. "I prefer the other chair," he said, trying to rouse a smile from Alec. It worked for a fleeting moment.

"The other one was more your era," Alec said.

"Always having a dig at my age," Cronin said wistfully. "One day you shall be a thousand years old and I'll remind you of this."

"I might be a thousand," Alec agreed, "but you'll be two thousand. Geriatric, by anyone's standards."

Cronin gasped, faking horror. He put his hand to his heart. "You wound me, m'cridhe."

Kennard was first to come back, declaring what Alec already knew. There was nothing here. Eiji and Jodis came back next, and while they bickered and joked about getting Cronin his very own throne, Alec wandered down to the burial tombs and the stained glass windows behind them.

He studied them, taking in the highest frames, which a human would need a twenty foot ladder to do. And he found something reoccurring throughout the Miracle Windows.

"Cronin," he murmured.

They stopped their joking and joined him in front of the magnificent stained glass windows. "Alec, what is it?"

He nodded toward the highest window. "Second frame from the top, in each section, can you see that?"

There in fragments of colored glass, each over eight hundred years old, was a knight with a lion blazoned on his chest, spearing a blackened devilish creature. No doubt thought to be symbolic of the slaying of evil, Alec saw it for what it was.

The blackened, devilish creature had a wolf-like face, complete with a muzzle full of sharp teeth, razor-like talons, and wings.

"Zoan," Cronin whispered.

Alec nodded. "Yes."

"What is the age of these windows?" Eiji asked.

"Twelfth century," Kennard answered.

"There might not be stone gargoyles here, but we're on the right track," Jodis said. She smiled at Alec, clearly happy at some kind of development. "This is good."

"He looks like Saint George," Alec noted. "And each man spearing a creature has the lion on his chest. Is that to depict the British monarchy or to ward off evil vampires?"

"Saint George is the patron saint of the Royal Family," Kennard said.

"To protect them from those dragon-like creatures?" Alec asked. "The Zoan?"

Kennard looked up at the stained glass windows. He took a moment to answer. "Possibly."

"Where to next?" Cronin asked.

"Rochester Cathedral," Kennard replied.

"These glass pictorials resemble Saint George," Eiji said. "Shouldn't we be going to Saint George's Cathedral?"

"Saint George's Cathedral wasn't built until the 1800s," Kennard told them. He looked back up at the windows.

"There'll be no such histories as these. And Rochester was built even before this place."

Alec nodded. "To Rochester Cathedral then. You know, I read books about this once. Dan Brown made a fortune. Maybe I should start writing this shit down."

Kennard laughed but the others didn't get the reference. Alec sighed. "Never mind."

Alec leapt them this time and landed them in the main aisle of the nave. The first thing he saw was the pulpitum screen statues: religious men carved from stone, perched eerily on the wall. "I have a healthy distrust of stone statues," Alec said. "After Egypt and China...." He shuddered. "Look at them! They're creepy as hell."

The church itself wasn't too bad, less foreboding somehow, but still, Alec felt a general sense of unease.

Cronin put his hand on Alec's arm. "Alec, are you well?"

"Yeah, I'm okay," he said. He shuddered again. "Something's not right, though."

Eiji spun on his heel, instantly on guard. "Which direction?"

"No one is here," Alec said. "But I can sense something. I don't know what it is. Down below us."

"The crypt," Cronin said. He put his hands on Alec and Kennard. Jodis and Eiji, who were centuries-used to Cronin's ways, reached out, and they found themselves in the crypt.

"I also have a healthy loathing of underground pits and tunnels," Alec mumbled.

Eiji and Jodis disappeared and returned a moment later. "Completely empty. There's nothing here."

Alec didn't know how he knew; he just did. He walked over to the far western wall, an area that was cordoned off to the public. It was natural bedrock with the numbers 1080—or the year, to be exact—carved into the stone. Alec looked at Cronin. "Was that you?"

Cronin snorted. "Defacing church walls, or graffiti for that matter, is not my style. Even back then."

Alec looked at Eiji. "You totally would."

Eiji nodded but looked at the inscription. "Yes, but this is not mine."

Alec laughed and put his hand on the wall, he closed his eyes and breathed. "There's something behind here."

"It's a solid stone wall," Jodis said. "Isn't it?"

Alec shook his head. "Do you trust me enough to leap us all in there?"

"Leap into a stone wall?" Kennard asked.

"Behind it," Alec elaborated. "I can sense it. I don't know how. A sense of space or something. There's a void. A cave."

Cronin nodded. "I trust you implicitly."

Eiji and Jodis nodded, and Kennard sighed dramatically. "Fine."

Alec closed his eyes and pictured the space in the rock wall and leapt them all there. It was a room all right. It was huge with a low ceiling and completely made from stone. There was no way in, no way out, impossibly hand carved. The ground seemed to have a circular design etched into the stone. But that wasn't the most disconcerting thing.

In the middle of the room in pointed formation stood five stone statues. They were as tall as Alec with cloaks of sandstone covering them from head to foot, their faces lowered and half-obscured, their feet tethered to the stone floor with heavy, rusted chains. But there was no mistaking what they were.

A cacophony of hisses came from Cronin, Eiji, Jodis,

and Kennard, all poised and ready for a fight. Alec threw out a protective shield around them, but the statues never moved.

Using one of his many talents, Alec got a sense of their true being. "They were Zoan. They're stone now."

Eiji stepped forward, and crouching down, looked up into the cloaked face. With a sharp gasp, he staggered backwards.

Then in a nanosecond, before Eiji could even hit the ground, Alec threw out his hands. The stone Zoan statues exploded into a mist of dust. Alec mentally grabbed everyone in the room, and he leapt.

CHAPTER NINE

THEY LANDED in the middle of their apartment in New York, just as they'd been in the stone room. Cronin had his hand out to Alec, Jodis was reaching for Eiji, Eiji was falling on his ass, and Alec had one hand raised to where the stone statues had been and his other arm out protecting Kennard.

Their sudden appearance, even with the one second warning from Eleanor, had sent Jacques into battle mode. He was on his feet, ready, standing in front of Kole, protecting him.

"We're fine," Alec declared quickly, sending a wave of calm over the room. "We're all good."

Cronin was quick to embrace Alec regardless, and with his arms around Alec, he turned to look at Eiji. "What the hell was that? What did you see?"

"Its eyes moved," Eiji said, swiftly getting to his feet. "Took me by surprise, which is something that doesn't happen often. I was not expecting that. Sorry."

Using his ability to pluck through memories, Alec saw what Eiji did. The creature's face was all teeth and looked just like a gargoyle, but its eyes of stone glinted and looked directly at Eiji. Eiji's visual perception skewed as he recoiled, and even through the shock and alarm, Alec could taste Eiji's need to get to his feet to defend and protect his friends.

That was why Alec adored him. Eiji was honest and as honorable as could be. He left the warmth of Cronin's embrace and gave Eiji a quick hug. "We don't need to worry about them anymore," Alec told him. "I turned them to dust." Alec went to his father next, clapping Jacques on the shoulder as he did. "You okay, Dad?"

"I'm fine," Kole replied. "It's not me I'm worried about. You saw more of those creatures?"

Alec gave a nod. "In a cave-like room built into bedrock under a church. They were gargoyles made of stone, yet they moved."

"Like the Terracotta soldiers moved when in your presence," Kennard said. "In the museum, those statues became animated too, Alec."

"What is it with your blood, Alec?" Kole asked. "I thought it would be different now, you know, now that *you're* different."

"Now that I'm vampire?" Alec asked rhetorically. "So did I."

"It seems the key is exactly that, a key. Vampire, human, it doesn't matter," Jodis said.

"That room the Zoan were imprisoned in," Cronin said, "had no entry or exit. It was simply a hole somehow carved into stone. How is that even possible?"

"Were they turned to stone and leapt there?" Eiji offered. "Maybe to warn or threaten other Zoan? How the room was made, or why they were chained to the floor, I cannot say."

The room was silent for a moment. Kennard looked at Alec and Cronin. "What now?"

"We go to France, as originally planned," Alec answered. "I think England gave us some answers, but I think the truth is in Paris."

"I agree," Cronin said. "Though it will be morning there soon. We should use this time to rest and research."

Alec hadn't realized how tired he was until Cronin mentioned it. He was still getting used to his vampire energy, and it was easy to forget that it had been days since he slept. Having such immeasurable powers was exhilarating, yes. Sometimes it felt like he could run and never stop, yet his powers were also taxing. His body needed rest, even if his mind never stopped.

And seeing how tired Kole looked made Alec stop. "Yes, I think that's a good idea." He looked to his father. "It's midnight, Dad. You should be in bed too."

"I was waiting for you to get back," he replied quietly.

Alec sighed. "Sit with me?"

They sat on the sofa and the other vampires in the room —despite being able to hear every word anyway—left to give them some privacy, except for Cronin. Alec asked him to stay. "There's something I need to ask," Alec said. "I don't need an answer right now. In fact, I'd rather you think about it."

Kole was concerned. "What is it, Alec?"

"From our meeting with Jorge and all this talk of mortality and the afterlife," Alec said, "well, that got me thinking...."

Kole smiled. "I wondered when you were gonna ask me this."

Alec could see in his father's mind that he knew what

Alec was asking. "If you were to be changed into a vampire, you could live forever."

Oh, Alec, son, Kole thought fondly. *No, that's not a life for me.*

Alec saw his father's answer, but it was something he needed to ask anyway. "I don't want to lose you, Dad."

"You won't," Kole said with a teary smile. "Use that perfect recall you got going on in that head of yours, and you can see me crystal clear."

"It won't be the same."

"No," Kole said. "It won't. But Alec, you can't have eternal life without facing death every so often."

"Cronin said something similar."

Kole smiled at Cronin. "He's a smart man."

Alec nodded and had to swallow the lump in his throat. "It won't be the same, Dad. You've been my one true rock, ya know? No matter what, you were always there."

"'Course I was," he said softly. "You're my son. Where else would I be?"

"That's why I need you to say yes," Alec said, fighting tears. The emotions of knowing he would one day lose his father overwhelmed him.

Kole shook his head slowly. "That's not my fate, son."

"I can't do forever knowing you're gone."

"You have to. Like every person who loses their parents, Alec. It's the natural order."

"But it doesn't have to be," Alec tried again. A single tear ran down his face.

Kole wouldn't be swayed. "Alec, I'll have my life and I'll not regret a minute. I'll go to my grave knowing you live on, and that right there is enough for me."

Alec started to cry and Kole pulled him in close. Alec cried into his neck, the way he did as a small boy. "I'm not gonna die just yet." Then Kole froze. "Am I? Have you seen it?"

Alec shook his head. "I won't look. I don't want to know. I don't ever want to know."

"Death and taxes, Alec. Can't avoid either of them," Kole said. "Oh shit, that reminds me. I have to fill out my tax forms."

Alec laughed despite his tears. He pulled back and wiped his cheeks with the back of his hands. "Oh, Dad."

"What?" Kole asked with a smile. "I'd prefer to face a pack of those Zoan creatures than the IRS."

Alec sat back on the sofa and sighed. He squeezed his father's hand. "I had to ask, Dad. But I will respect your wishes."

"I know you had to ask, Alec," Kole said. "But when I do go, don't be sad. Remember a life well lived. Be happy that I died knowing I raised you right."

Alec swallowed hard. "Thanks, Dad." He took a moment to collect himself and to bask in the love of both men beside him.

Are you well, m'cridhe? Cronin asked.

Alec gave him a nod. *I am. Disappointed but fine.* After a moment of silence, Alec thought of something. "Dad," Alec started, "we need to go to Europe."

"I know."

"I want you to come with us," Alec said.

Kole was clearly surprised. "What for?"

"Don't you want to see it?" Alec asked. "The Eiffel Tower, Notre Dame... the old churches, the history...."

"The history, yes," Kole said. "Those Zoan creatures, not at all."

"You'll be protected with us," Alec tried. "Jacques will need to come with us. And he's sworn to guard you, Dad."

Kole frowned. "I'll be okay here."

Alec nodded but couldn't help the disappointment that showed clearly on his face. "Okay."

Kole sat back on the sofa, looking older than Alec ever remembered. "What's the real reason you want me to go?"

"I want to spend time with you," Alec admitted softly. "I worry, that's all." He was quiet a moment, then added, "And I'm busy all the time, and I don't want you to feel excluded. I miss you, and I thought you'd like to see some of Europe. You've never been, and it's something I can give you." Alec sighed heavily. "I just want to spend time with you."

"Oh, Alec," Kole whispered. He put his hand on Alec's knee. "If it means that much to you, then I'll go. But be warned, I'm old and I'll slow you down."

"I'll leap you back here at the first sign of trouble," Alec told him. "It's not all bad, Dad. You'll see some amazing things as well."

Kole patted his knee, then stood up with a groan. "Better put this old body to bed then."

"Night, Dad."

Cronin gave Kole a nod, and Alec knew Cronin was watching him as he watched his dad walk out of the room. It amazed him still to see himself through Cronin's eyes. It was intense and humbling.

Alec?

Alec looked at Cronin then and gave him a smile. *Hey.*

Are you well?

Alec loved it when Cronin asked him that. *I am. How about you?*

You are worried about your father?

Alec let out a slow breath. *He's human... mortal.*

Oh, m'cridhe.

I will miss him.

Cronin frowned, his chest filled with a hollow ache at Alec's grief, which, of course, Alec's empathic ability let him feel. Cronin stood up and held out his hand. "To bed."

In that very moment, Alec didn't want anything more. With a nod, he took Cronin's hand and allowed him to lead them to their room. He shut the door, shutting out the world, and took Alec's face in his hands. Cronin kissed his cheeks, his closed eyelids, his lips. *Loss is never easy.*

I don't want him to die.

Cronin pushed Alec's hair from his forehead and stared into his eyes. *Your sadness is a weight in my heart.*

"I'm sorry," Alec whispered. The bond between fated lovers meant they each felt the pain of their mate.

Cronin scoffed with half a smile. *Don't apologize, m'cridhe, for it is a burden I willingly shoulder with you. I wish I could carry it for you.*

Alec melted against him, and Cronin wrapped his arms around him. *You carry me more than you know.*

Cronin slid his hand along Alec's jaw and kissed him softly. Then, still fully dressed, he laid Alec on the bed and pulled off his shoes. Then he took off his own shoes and climbed in beside him. Cronin dragged the covers up, pulled Alec in tight against him, and kissed the side of his head. "Sleep, m'cridhe. *Rug mi ort.*"

Alec inhaled deeply and tightened his hold on Cronin. Those words soothed him still. *I have you, too.*

CRONIN WOKE SUDDENLY, his arms still around Alec. Before he could wonder what startled him, Alec flinched again in his sleep. He fussed and mumbled and flinched again. "No," he whispered, still deep asleep.

Cronin traced his fingers through Alec's hair. "Alec?"

He mumbled again, words Cronin couldn't decipher. And then Cronin felt it, a bloom of unease and fear. He knew it was coming from Alec, his empathic talent radiating from him, even as he slept. A bad dream, Cronin realized, as uncommon as it was for a vampire to dream, would be harmless enough. For a normal vampire. But Alec wasn't normal. Every known vampire talent bubbled under the surface, and in his sleep, Alec didn't seem aware his powers were affecting the real world.

"Alec!" Cronin said, louder this time. The emotions Alec was radiating twisted in Cronin's gut. He shook his shoulder to try and wake him. Alec struggled this time, still asleep, and mumbled incoherently.

"Alec!"

The bedroom door opened and Eiji and Jodis stood, clearly concerned. "What's wrong?"

"He won't wake up," Cronin said. He got to his knees on the bed and shook Alec harder. "Alec!"

Alec shot upright, hands out, and with a plume of energy, he sent Cronin hurtling off the bed. Cronin's back hit the wall, knocking a dent into the drywall, and Eiji and Jodis made a start toward him.

Alec startled again, realizing what he'd done, and this time, he threw out his hand, fingers spread wide. "Stop!"

And everything stopped.

Everything.

Except for Cronin and Alec, but Eiji and Jodis were in mid-step, their hair splayed out behind them, as though captured in a photograph.

"Alec," Cronin whispered. "What did you just do?"

He sat on the bed, blankets twisted around his waist. "I don't know," he whispered. He looked at Cronin, clearly trying to contain the fear that threatened to explode outward. "I don't know." And only then did he seem to realize that Cronin was on the floor, pushed against the wall. "Did I do that?" He became panicked and scrambled off the bed toward Cronin. "Did I hurt you?"

Cronin shook his head and stood up. He held his hand out for Alec, needing to touch him. Alec looked at the dent in the wall properly, then and flinched back from Cronin's touch. Then he looked at Eiji and Jodis, still frozen in time. It was the most frightened Cronin had ever seen him. Alec shook his head. "What have I done?"

Cronin pulled Alec roughly against him and held him fiercely, and as soon as he touched Alec, Eiji and Jodis came to life. They continued on their way around the bed to where Cronin was, but Eiji stopped when he realized Cronin wasn't where he was a split second ago. He put his arm out to stop Jodis and kept it there as if to protect her, then turned to where Cronin now stood at the bed holding Alec. "You didn't leap just now," he said. It wasn't a question.

Cronin shook his head. "No."

Jodis looked at Cronin, then at Alec, and seeing how scared they were, she was instantly on alert mode. "What just happened?"

Cronin tightened his hold on Alec. "I'm not sure. But I think Alec just stopped time."

ALEC SAT ON THE SOFA, quiet and lost. Cronin sat beside him, holding his hand. *I'm so sorry. I'm so sorry,* Alec kept thinking over and over, the words heartfelt and hurting.

Its okay, Alec, Cronin squeezed his hand. *You didn't mean to do it.*

I could have hurt you. I could have killed you.

Cronin shook his head. *No. You couldn't have. Alec, you were asleep.*

That's what makes it worse. Alec brought his knees up and folded into himself. *I had no control over what just happened.*

Alec, Cronin started to say.

"Can you tell us what happened?" Jodis said, not aware of Cronin and Alec's private conversation.

Alec shook his head. "Not really. I was dreaming.... I haven't dreamed since I was human," he whispered.

"Vampires don't normally dream," Jodis said, cautiously eyeing Cronin.

Alec shrugged one shoulder. His voice was quiet. "Just another thing to add to my freak list."

"You're not a freak," Cronin said, squeezing his hand so hard that if Alec were still human, he'd have crushed it.

Alec looked at Cronin, his eyes filled with tears. "I hurt you. I am so, so sorry."

Cronin shook his head. "Alec, I was not harmed."

"I threw you across the fucking room, Cronin." Alec clenched his jaw, but he squeezed Cronin's hand in return. He put his free hand to his heart. "I will never forgive myself."

Knowing no words would soothe him, Cronin put his forehead on Alec's shoulder and let his chest bloom with all the love he felt for him. He knew Alec could feel it, because his breath caught and he sniffed back tears. He pulled Alec against him, and Alec let himself be held, the fight in him gone.

Everyone in the room stood in silence, and Cronin was glad that Kole was still asleep. Alec was burdened enough with knowing his father's very human life was, in its brevity, not something he would have forever. He didn't need to have his father worry for him as well.

"Alec," Jodis said softly.

"Please," Cronin said gruffly. "Give us a moment."

"No," Alec mumbled, sitting up, though he kept a hold of Cronin's hand. "I'll show you what I saw, then we can try and figure out what the hell it was. I know I bitched and moaned about you cataloguing my talents, Jodis, but I promise you I'll do whatever it takes if it means I never hurt Cronin again."

Cronin was going to argue that he wasn't hurt, but didn't want to continue the argument. Instead, he said, "You can show them my memory, if you'd prefer. I saw everything."

Alec nodded and a moment later, he relayed what had happened in Cronin's mind into the minds of everyone in the room. They saw how Alec flinched in his sleep, they saw Cronin's concern trying to wake him. They saw Eiji and Jodis open the door, then they saw a very startled and distressed Alec expel an explosion of energy from his hands. They all witnessed how even though Cronin was blown backwards into the drywall, he wasn't hurt. His only concern was for Alec. And then of course, how Alec yelled to stop, and how Eiji and Jodis were frozen in mid-air until Cronin touched him, making time start again.

Everyone was quiet as they processed what they'd just witnessed. Cronin was the first to speak. "You see, Alec? I was not harmed. You were not at fault."

"I was dreaming," Alec explained quietly. "Jorge was in my dream. The Zoan were there, and Jorge was in immense pain. I don't know why. But then I woke up and you were against the wall, and Eiji and Jodis were running toward you. I had to protect you. I mean, I know, I *know* they'd never hurt you, but I was scared. My dream left me disoriented."

"I felt your fear," Cronin told him.

Alec stared at Cronin and whispered, "I had to protect you. I don't really remember what I did. I just needed to stop everything and get my bearings."

Jodis walked over and leaned down to put her hand on Alec's arm. "You stopped time, Alec. Yet Cronin remained unaffected." She smiled warmly at him. "This changes everything."

"Did you want me to try doing it again?" Alec asked. "We can run some more tests, like we've done for all the other talents. I don't know if I'll be able to recall the exact synapses that fired that talent, Jodis, but I will try."

Cronin knew that Jodis was well aware of how much Alec had grown to despise those tests, yet here he was willingly offering to do whatever it took. She shook her head. "Later. Go and spend some time together. I think you need it. Let us finish gathering what information we can find."

Cronin lifted Alec's chin so he would look at him. "Pick anywhere in the world, Alec, and I will take you. The field at Dunadd? A hotel room in Budapest? Anywhere you want."

"Just wherever you are," Alec said. "It doesn't matter. As long as we're together."

Cronin pressed his lips to Alec's forehead. He got their boots for them, and when they were ready, he announced, "We shan't be long." And they were gone.

CRONIN WATCHED Alec's face as he took in his surroundings. His mouth was open, his eyes wide, and he stood, turning in a slow circle, looking at the ceiling of ice above them. "Where exactly are we? I was expecting to see the battlefield at Dunadd."

"Breidamerkurjökull Glacier, Iceland," Cronin answered. He couldn't help but feel a little smug at the awe on Alec's face. If he wanted a distraction, this was the perfect choice.

Alec tilted his head and scanned the walls of crystal clear ice. "Wow. How did you even know about this place?"

"If you live long enough on this planet with the capability to go anywhere you want with a mere thought, it doesn't take long before you go, well, everywhere."

"Cronin, this place is magical."

Cronin laughed and the sound reverberated off the frozen wave walls. "If you were human, you'd have to trek and abseil to get down here. And given it is winter here, dressed in the clothes you're wearing, you'd have about fifteen minutes to live."

But Alec was right. It was spectacular. A truly wondrous sight.

"Those colors," Alec said, staring up at the ceiling of ice, "are from the Northern lights, yes?"

The slightest hints of green and blue refracted through the ice, it would have been undetectable to human eyes. "Yes," Cronin said. He held out his hand. "Let's walk."

They leapt easily over the smooth frozen floor, deeper into the caves beneath the glacier, and Cronin explained this glacier was older than even he was.

That made Alec laugh. "Please tell me you know of more hidden places."

Cronin stopped walking and pulled Alec into his arms. "I will show you every single one."

Alec tightened his hold on Cronin and sighed deeply against him. They didn't speak for a long while, and Cronin did his best to clear his mind. He knew Alec was constantly bombarded with the thoughts of others, so he did his best to give him peace. It earned him a soft kiss to the side of his head.

"Thank you," Alec murmured. *For bringing me here. For everything.*

"I figured you could use the remoteness," Cronin replied. "There isn't another mind to hear for many miles."

"I feel better already."

Cronin smiled and pulled back so he could kiss Alec softly. "I am glad."

"I am sorry about before," Alec said.

"I know you are, though your reasons are unwarranted."

"I'm sorry nonetheless."

Cronin kissed him again. "Did you want to talk about your dream?" When Alec didn't answer, Cronin prompted him. "It was of Jorge, yes?"

Alec nodded. His voice was quiet when he spoke, clearly still haunted by what he saw in his dream. "The Zoan were there, the five cloaked ones. He was in a world of pain—I've not felt anything like it. They held him in a circle of stones or a round room. I don't really know... it was unclear. Like the Callanish or Stonehenge, but not. That doesn't make sense...."

Cronin thought about what that could mean. "Do you think it was a prophecy?"

Alec stopped walking and waited for Cronin to look at him. "I do."

"Then we need to go to Jorge."

"Yes. If I use my talents and focus on Jorge, I can see that he's okay. He's with Adelmo in the jungle, and he's happy." Then Alec said, "But it felt very real. I know that vampires aren't supposed to dream at all, and given my mind is a universe of unknowns, I guess I shouldn't be surprised. But it was different than a vision of the future. I don't know, Cronin. It was strange."

"A Zoan trick of the mind, perhaps?" Cronin offered. "Testing your resolve at a subconscious level?"

Alec nodded slowly. "Possibly." He took a deep breath. "I can't help but think the shape is important. A circle. I don't know why or how. But I became a vampire with the power of the Callanish Standing Stones, which is circular. The Zoan came through a portal in the Göbekli Tepe, also a circle. It can't be a coincidence."

"Circular altars, circular rooms, circular sigils have been used throughout history for religions and sorcery," Cronin said. "If you believe that kind of thing."

"Or for bringing back vampires," Alec added. "I guess religion, sorcery, and the supernatural is all subjective to your beliefs."

Cronin offered him a small smile. "Perspective changes when faced with a different kind of mortality, does it not?"

"It does."

"Neither one is wrong or right."

"It's a little disconcerting, I have to admit."

"Agreed. That is why the discovery of the vampire afterworld is such an incredible find for me," Cronin told him. "My perspective on mortality, and even immortality, changes yet again. I still want forever with you. And I want *this* forever. Not the next."

Alec smiled, even though he'd not completely shaken off the horrible feeling from before. He took a deep breath and let it out slowly. "Not to mention the whole concept of time. If I can actually stop it, what does that make it? Time is an intangible concept, isn't it? Granted, it's a man-made concept, so what mankind has told itself to be an unbendable truth, is merely just a concept. No different to religion, I guess."

Cronin considered the reality of time not being a constant thing. Alec was right. Time was no more a gospel truth than any other thing humans have told themselves throughout history. "You know that Jodis will want you to practice your new ability to stop time," Cronin said, getting back to more recent events.

"Yeah. She thinks if I can stop time and keep you unfrozen, then we can beat the Zoan at their own game," Alec said. "Her thoughts are pretty clear."

"She only has your best interests at heart," Cronin added.

Alec snorted out a laugh. "You don't need to defend her. I know she's your best friend, but I can see her intentions are honest."

Cronin shook his head. "You're wrong."

"No, I'm pretty sure I'm not. I can see her thoughts, her meanings, objectives, the things she doesn't say out loud. She keeps a lot to herself, which some people should be thankful for, let me tell you, but she's as honorable as Eiji."

Cronin chuckled. "No. You're wrong about her being my best friend. Close friend, oldest friend, dearest maybe. But you are my best friend."

"Awww," Alec crooned. He kissed Cronin with smiling lips. "And you are mine."

Cronin took his time, gently cupping Alec's face and kissing him properly. Not a kiss that was leading to anything more, just a perfect kiss. When they pulled apart, he rested his forehead on Alec's. "We should be going back."

Alec closed his eyes and smiled. "Thank you for bringing me here. I needed peace and quiet, and you somehow knew that without me saying so."

"Anytime, m'cridhe," Cronin whispered.

THE APARTMENT in New York City was buzzing. Research books were still out, laptop screens with a dozen different Internet tabs were open, and a few more details had been added to the whiteboard. If it resembled a special ops confab, then Jodis was clearly the commanding officer.

How Alec could tune out not only the mental voices in the room, but those of the closest few million people in the City, Cronin would never know. He'd likened the control of his many talents once to having a hundred tabs open on an Internet browser and simply muting one. It seemed incomprehensible to Cronin, yet Alec did it with ease.

Well, normally he did. Today was a little difficult.

"Can you give me a minute?" he asked of Eiji, who had hit him with a dozen quick-fired questions. Alec sat down on the sofa, closed his eyes, and was eerily still. Before Cronin could ask what he was doing, Alec opened his eyes and smiled. "Jorge and Adelmo," he said softly, and in the next second, Jorge and Adelmo appeared in the living room.

"Alec!" Jorge cried and ran over to him, smiling from ear

to ear. He jumped onto his lap. Adelmo seemed a little more reserved.

"Please, sit down and I'll explain," Alec told him. Alec waited for Adelmo to sit on the sofa, then he explained, not just for Adelmo but for everyone. "I sought the mind of Jorge here," Alec said, giving the boy a tickle and making him laugh, "and asked if I could leap them here."

"Importante," Jorge said.

"Yes, it's important," Alec went on to say. He looked at Adelmo when he spoke next. "I had a dream, or a vision came to me while I slept—I'm not sure which it was—that Jorge was in danger." Alec explained his dream of the Zoan. "They threatened me before, and now I believe they mean to include Jorge."

Adelmo hissed and his eyes narrowed.

Alec put out a small wave of calm to pacify him. "I know. This is why I asked you here. We can protect him better here. All of us."

Jorge looked up to Alec, his brown eyes inquisitive but sad. "Why Jorge?"

Alec shrugged. "I don't know. But I'd rather you stayed here with us until we know you're safe, okay?"

"How does the key not know?" Jorge asked.

"Apparently I can't see these creatures unless they show themselves to me," Alec answered. "I can't see anything about them."

"The same ones you ask Jorge about before?"

Alec nodded but it was Cronin who spoke. "Jorge, have you seen anything else, from the people who talk to you? Alec's mother or Willem? Have they shown you anything else?"

Jorge shook his head. "*Nada más.*"

Nothing else.

"Could you ask them?" Cronin pressed. "*Por favor.*"

"Cronin is worried," Jorge said, looking up at Alec.

Alec smiled at Cronin, then at Jorge. "He is. I am too. I don't want anyone to hurt you."

It had been horrifying for Adelmo when Jorge was taken, leapt from his home and held captive in the underground pits of China. Alec had explained that he could see the paternal bond Adelmo had with Jorge, and now Cronin wondered if Alec somehow felt responsible.

Alec's gaze shot to Cronin. *Of course I do. How could I not? He's a child, albeit a vampire, but still just a kid. We should protect him, all of us.*

Cronin fought a smile. *You're a good man, Alec.*

Vampire.

Same thing.

"Are you two done?" Eiji was smiling at them. He must have thought something next because Alec laughed.

"Jorge look for you, look for you, he will," Jorge said in the riddled way he spoke.

"Muchas gracias," Alec said. Then he looked up at Cronin and was serious again. "Dad will be awake soon. We'd better get ready for Paris."

"We have the coven meeting tonight," Jodis reminded them.

"We'll be back by then," Alec said with a nod.

"Jodis?" Eiji asked. "Are you not coming with us?"

"I will stay here," she replied softly to him. "I will have as much information together for the meeting tonight as I can, and I will stay to keep watch over Jorge."

"If you are sure." Eiji looked torn, and it was not a sight Cronin liked to see.

Alec either, apparently. He walked over to Jodis and put his hand on her shoulder. "I'm transferring the talent of leaping to you. It will only last until I get back, but if you need to, you can hightail it outta here, okay? Just think of somewhere safe and you'll be there."

Jodis rolled her eyes, as though Alec lacked faith in her ability to defend the vampires staying behind. But Eiji was happier with this development, and the small smile she gave him told Cronin that Jodis was too.

"Kennard and Jacques will be with us," Cronin said. "And Kole, so that makes six."

Eleanor stepped forward. She'd been so quiet Cronin had almost forgotten she was there. "For what it's worth," she said, "I foresee no problems. I know we cannot see the Zoan creatures, but you will all be at the coven meeting tonight, if that is of any consolation."

Alec walked over and gave her a quick hug, surprising her. "Thank you, Eleanor."

"What for?" she mumbled. "I've never felt so useless."

"You are far from useless," Alec said warmly. "You've helped us numerous times. Just because I have the seer talent doesn't mean you're not needed. When I am gone, you can see any imminent danger and Jodis can leap you all out, okay?"

"I cannot see the Zoan."

Alec shrugged. "Neither can I. So we're as useless as each other."

Eleanor gasped, looking somewhat horrified. "You're not useless, Alec."

"Some would argue," Kole said, his voice still rough from sleeping.

Alec smiled at him. "Morning, Dad. Ready for our big day?"

"Need a cup of tea first," he grumbled without stopping and walked straight into the kitchen.

Eiji snorted out a laugh. "Reminds me of you, Alec, when you were human. It was coffee or someone would die."

Alec scrunched up his nose. "Even the thought of drinking coffee now makes my stomach turn."

"What about steak?" Eiji said with a grin.

"Only if it's rare," Kole chimed in from the kitchen. "If the blood runs out of it."

Everyone laughed. Alec's mouth fell open and he gawped toward the kitchen. "Dad!"

Kole appeared in the doorway, holding a steaming teacup in both hands. Eleanor had already brewed his tea. He shrugged and sipped his drink. "Just tellin' it like it is, son." Then he looked around the room and realized Jorge and Adelmo were there. He turned back to Alec. "So, what did I miss?"

"Have your breakfast, Dad. Get showered. I'll tell you everything when we get to Paris."

CHAPTER TEN

LEAPING into a dark and cold alley was nothing new to vampires, but Kole wasn't too familiar. He hated leaping, and Cronin deduced the effect on the older man's body was worse. Alec kept him close and pulsed a wave of pain relief through him.

"You okay?" Alec asked him.

"Yeah, yeah," Kole said, trying to downplay it. "Though I'd take a ten hour plane trip over leaping any day." He looked up at the stone walls at their sides. "Are we really in Paris?"

Cronin looked up and down the deserted street. There were cars parked and sounds of the city, but no one was in view. "This is Rue Massillon," he said with perfect French inflections. "If you look to your left," he nodded up the dark street, and at the end was a well-lit huge stone building. "That is Notre Dame."

Kole pulled his coat collar up around his ears. He huffed. "Well, then I guess leaping isn't all bad."

Jacques laughed quietly. "Paris is my old stomping ground. Though I like New York as well." His French accent seemed stronger here. "Come, Kole. I will show you some sights."

They walked down the street to where the Notre Dame Cathedral hulked over them in all its Gothic architectural glory. The stone building was dark and wet, adding to the eeriness as they walked up Rue de Cloître Notre Dame, rounding the corner to the front of the building. The five of them stood back, looking up at the towers, taking in the magnificent sight before them.

"The gargoyles," Kennard said softly. "Look at them."

"Yeah," Eiji agreed. "They look very familiar."

"Look at the stained glass window," Alec said. "In the third segment."

Cronin recognized them immediately. They were the same devilish creatures depicted in the stained glass windows in London. Black winged creatures, somewhat resembling a dragon-type wolf being speared by a knight. They were the same creatures that now stood as stone statues on the very walls they were looking at. "Zoan."

"You can see that?" Kole whispered. "I mean, seriously? I can barely make out the window. I can see the window is round."

Eiji snorted. "Kole, you are so much like Alec."

Alec smiled, then nodded toward the tower, to where the infamous gargoyles were perched. "I think we should check out the crypt first. That is why we're here, but I also want to go up there afterwards. Something's telling me to get a closer look at the gargoyles." Then he looked around and saw just how visible they all were, even at three in the morning, so leaping directly wasn't an option. "There are too many eyes. Let's go back to the alley."

Alec stopped in a small alcove, Cronin presumed, when he was sure they were out of view from any humans.

"Ready?" And the next minute the six of them were four stories below the streets of Paris, even under the belly of Notre Dame.

THE SPACE they were in was completely black, and Alec felt the immediate fear run through his father of being buried alive. Alec immediately sent out some balls of light, or lumen, so that Kole could see. Kole wasn't wrong though. It was like an underground cave with a low dirt ceiling. There seemed to be tunnels leading off into obscured darkness, but in the center of the space were hollowed out circular pits with stone pillars erected at the circumference of the center circle.

"Jesus," Alec said. "Nine circles. "

"Ah Alec, this is not the vault of Notre Dame," Eiji said, taking in the view before him.

"No, we're underneath even that," he said. "Humans haven't found these yet."

Cronin took a deep breath. "It looks like another portal."

Eiji agreed. He jumped into the center pit and scooped up a handful of dirt from the ground. He let it fall through his hand and shook his head. "Nothing has been here in a long time."

"I don't like it," Alec said. Then he said, low enough so only the vampires could hear, "And neither does my father." Kole was a white shade of pale, so Alec sent him a quick dose of calm. At least it got his heart rate down a little.

"Let's go," Cronin said, giving Kole a smile. "I've seen enough. Let's go check out some stone statues."

Alec didn't hesitate, and a moment later, they stood in the left tower of Notre Dame.

"Whoa," Kole mumbled, putting his hands out to balance himself.

Alec was quick to put his arm around him. "You're fine, Dad. It's safe here. And look at that," Alec said, stepping aside so Kole could see the view.

The Eiffel Tower stood proud and illuminated over the city of Paris. "Oh, wow," Kole mumbled. "Yes, this is much better."

Kennard moaned. "Lord, I detest the French." He looked at Jacques. "No offense."

Jacques rolled his eyes, and ignoring him, pointed out some visible landmarks to Kole.

Eiji barked out a laugh. "Kennard, you don't like anyone that's not English."

Kennard straightened and sniffed indignantly. "True."

Cronin couldn't help but laugh. Kennard was oddly still a monarchist, even as a vampire. It wasn't that he was prejudiced toward others—he loved his friends from all over the world fiercely—he was just staunchly all for Queen and country and heckled everyone else like he was supporting a football team.

"Detest them more than the Scottish?" Alec asked with a smile.

Kennard made a face as though he couldn't decide and shrugged. "Not including their Irish counterparts."

Eiji laughed. "Never did get over the Irish rebellion, did you?"

Kennard glowered, and Cronin clapped him on the arm. "Ah, the French helping the Irish. The good old days."

Then in a flash, a protective shield went up around them and Alec had moved from Cronin's side to be in front of them. His hands were out as if holding some different force only he could see, his fangs bared, before any of the others had blinked.

Everyone was immediately on the defensive, with Kole in the protected center. "What is it?" Cronin hissed.

But then he saw it.

The infamous gargoyles that graced the walls of Notre Dame had moved. These stone creatures had turned their heads and were now staring at them, or more specifically, they were staring at Alec.

The closest one, the one that resembled a winged wolf, opened its mouth. No sound came out, just a scraping of stone on stone. Then it moved its wings, stretching them, but it was slow and grating. The noise was unnatural, the movements seemed protracted and painful, and then the creature finally let out a scratchy yowl. It set the other gargoyles into motion.

Another one, more dragon-like, with a muzzle full of eroded teeth, a long neck, and claws came scratching up and over the wall. It made a scraping, screeching scream as it came at them.

"Alec?" Jacques hissed. He was now standing in front of Kole, shielding him.

Alec threw out his hands, turning both stone creatures into a mist of dust. Then another one, and one more, until one by one, Alec rendered them to dust. Some were misshapen, some half eroded; time and rain had left its mark, but yet they still moved.

"Wait," Alec whispered. Two more gargoyles crept closer. Teeth bared, claws out, closer and closer....

"Alec," Kennard said, his voice sharp with warning.

"Wait," Alec repeated. Then all the gargoyles popped,

exploding into dust where they stood. All of them. Even the ones still mounted on the walls.

"What did you just do?" Eiji asked. He ran to the edge of the tower and looked up and down the exterior walls. "They're all gone."

"I needed to get a sense of them," Alec explained, following Eiji to the edge. "Once I could grasp them all in my mind, I could take them all out at once." He could see the once very famous gargoyles that sat for two centuries were now gone. "The uh, the media is going to be all over this come sunup."

Then, across the city, a shrill scream cried out, then one more, and then another. Human screams, and at the early hour, the sound was chilling. It was panicked, hysterical cries from both men and women. The five vampires all turned to the direction the cries carried from, though Kole clearly couldn't hear it. Before anyone could ask what would cause such a thing, a shrill squawk cut through the night air.

It was a screeching, stone scraping on stone sound, and there was no doubt then what could have made it.

Alec wrapped his arms around his father and leapt them all to the source of the noise. They appeared outside the Musée d'Orsay. Peppered with dim external wall lighting and the ambient streetlights which lined the Seine River, the view would've caused Cronin to pause at its beauty on any other night. But that was not what caught his attention.

A large wolf-looking stone creature spun on its heel and hissed at them. It narrowed its eyes at Alec and gnashed its teeth, hulking down like it was stalking prey. Some people, mostly homeless people and sex-workers, ran screaming from them as the creature opened its huge mouth. Its chest glowed yellow and orange, and Cronin knew it was about to breathe fire.

Alec must have thought the same thing, or perhaps he could see into the creature's mind. Cronin didn't know. But as the creature sucked back a breath, its chest glowed orange to red, and as it was about to exhale flames, Alec put both his hands out and yelled, "Stop!"

And everything froze.

The world around them stopped except for the vampires. The creature stood like the stone it was made from, frozen in time. Kole too and the other humans running, caught mid-stride, like they were in a photograph.

"Holy shit," Kennard whispered, looking around. His eyes were like saucers, his mouth open. "Alec?"

"You stopped time," Eiji said, with just as much wonder as Kennard.

Cronin looked at the stone creature. "If this one came to life with the others, then it's safe to assume it's not the only one."

Eiji nodded. "Yes. Though the question is, was it just gargoyles in this vicinity? Maybe all of Paris? Or all of the world?" Eiji walked over to the stone lycan-looking animal and hesitatingly put his hand to its still-red chest. "It's very hot."

Kennard's eyebrows shot up. "Jesus." He turned to Alec, as if to ask him something, but Alec wasn't paying them any mind.

For Alec couldn't take his eyes off his father. Kole stood shocked and pale with his hand up, frozen in time; his eyes were unseeing, no breath came from his lips. Alec raised his hand slowly and put it to Kole's face. Jacques stood to the side, never far from Kole. He was his sworn protector, and he did his job well. But even he could see Alec needed a moment with his father.

"Alec?" Cronin slid his hand along Alec's back. He looked again at Kole, and he could feel Alec's anguish as though it were his own emotion. "He's alive, just stopped with time. That's all. He's fine."

Alec nodded. "But for how long?"

Cronin put his forehead on Alec's shoulder, knowing there was no answer that would appease him. Not for this. His father was human and therefore mortal. His life, on a timeline such as Cronin's, was brief, and Cronin knew the scar Alec would bear at the loss of his father would last an eternity. So no, there were no words to soothe a looming grief, but he wanted Alec to know he was not alone.

Kennard and Eiji studied the stone creature, lightly touching it.

"Don't get too close," Cronin warned. "I don't know how long the time lapse will last."

Alec looked around then, and with no more than a slight nod of his head, the huge stone statue fell to dust. It smoldered on the cobblestone, the heat still resonating within the ashes, though they quickly died away.

Eiji looked between Alec and Kole, and gave Alec a sad smile. "Alec, I hate to ask this of you right now, but can you get a sense of any other gargoyles that may have come to life?"

Alec closed his eyes. "I can't see the whole city. It's too big an area. But there are some others...." His eyelids flickered. "Well, there were. They're now dust."

"We should notify Gautier," Cronin said. The elder of the Parisian coven should be made aware, if he was not already.

Alec closed his eyes and took a deep breath. Cronin

assumed he was using his mental tracking ability to seek the elder out, but then his eyes shot open. "Gautier's stopped with time as well. They all have."

Eiji raised an eyebrow. "It seems those not affected are with you when you stop time."

Alec shrugged. "Or I haven't got a handle on it yet. I don't know. It's very strange, even to me."

"How do you restart it?" Kennard asked. He turned around and looked around the stock-still street. "As much as I'd like to explore this reality we are seeing, I'd like to know if it's permanent or just fleeting? Though if you plan on doing it again, maybe next time I could bring a British flag to grace the Eiffel Tower?" His eyes lit up with the possibilities. "Oh yes, that would be fabulous."

Eiji snorted out a laugh but it was short lived. "As mildly entertaining as watching World War III break out between England and France would be, Kennard, I'd like to get home to my Jodis, and see she is unharmed, if that's okay."

Alec looked at his father for a long moment. "Yeah," he whispered. "As tempting as it is, we can't stay like this. Though I'm not sure how to restart—"

Then Alec gasped in shock. Like an explosion, time popped back into reality, the world started turning again, and the five vampires were jolted from their feet. They all staggered back a step, but Cronin reached out for Alec. "What was it?"

"I saw them," he whispered. "I can see the Zoan when time is stopped."

Kole looked around, scratching his head, thoroughly confused. "When time's what?" He looked up the street. "Where did that stone lycan go? Did you get it?"

Alec nodded. "Yeah, Dad. We got it." He swallowed hard and looked right at Cronin. "I saw them!"

Cronin gave a hard nod. "We need to leave. We've had enough witnesses tonight."

Kennard looked up at the lampposts and nodded to one. "There are CCTV cameras here too. They will have seen everything."

"Fuck," Alec cursed. He looked at the few people who were still in the street who hadn't run off. With no more than a soft breath from Alec, the humans all blinked in unison. "They won't remember us," he said. "But I can't do much about live video feeds." He shook his head. "Let's go."

THEY ARRIVED BACK in New York to find the others oblivious to the halt in time. It seemed to Cronin that only those vampires near Alec at the exact moment he stopped time remained unaffected. This was a good development, according to Jodis, and she was quick to document the finding in her catalogues.

"I can see the Zoan when I stop time," Alec said. "When we were in that reality in that time slip, I saw them. I couldn't see them before, but I did this time."

"Are you becoming more adept?" Jodis wondered. "Or has something changed?"

Alec shrugged. "I don't know."

"What did you see?" Eleanor asked.

"There were five of them," Alec explained. "They had their cloaks pulled back and they had no human skins. The Zoan look like lycan. Some had wings, some didn't."

"Just like gargoyles," Cronin said.

Alec nodded. "I'll show you what I saw."

Then in Cronin's mind he saw them. They did look like wolves standing upright, with grotesque features and horrific teeth and claws. They were in a stone room, like a wet and gray cell. They seemed unaware that Alec could see them. It was a fleeting glance, but it was real.

"*Cárcel de piedra*," Jorge said. The little boy was excited.

Alec stared at him for a long second. "Yes. Stone prison."

Jodis nodded. "It did look like a cell."

Cronin agreed. "But can we see where? Are they even on our time? Do they even exist in our reality or do they cross over somehow when our time stops?"

"When they stop time," Alec said. "When they stop it, they control it. It seems when I stop it, I control it?" He shook his head. "I don't know. I wish I had more answers than questions."

"Uh, guys?" Kennard called out. "You might wanna come see this." He was at the dining table with two laptops open. "The Internet has gone berserk."

Alec sighed deeply. "Yeah. There were cameras in the street," he said for those who weren't there. "I failed at minimizing the human witnesses, including surveillance, and I take full responsibility."

"Alec, you are not to blame for that," Cronin said quickly. "You saved those people."

"Uh, it's not that exactly," Kennard added. He turned the laptop around to face the others and pressed a video clip. There was footage from all over Paris of stone statues, gargoyles ripping free from their mountings and scampering down walls. There was footage of these lycan-type gargoyles chasing people in the darkened streets, a clip of one such creature flapping its stone wings and breathing out a rush of fire, people running, people screaming. Then there was more footage of all these horrifying creatures simply falling to dust as they ran.

Alec scrubbed his hand over his face. "Jesus Christ."

Then finally the CCTV footage from in front of the Musée d'Orsay. It showed the huge stone lycan-looking creature chasing two women before six people suddenly appeared from nowhere. It showed Alec throwing out his hands. The footage flickered for a moment, and when it came back on, the creature was gone, and in its place was a smoldering pile of dust and ash. The six people who had magically appeared were unsteady on their feet like an earthquake hit, then a moment later, they disappeared into thin air.

The audio to the clip was from a French news station. "The person wanted for questioning by police has been identified as ex-New York Detective, Alec MacAidan. The same man who was seen on surveillance footage eighteen months ago disappearing from a New York City police precinct headquarters with this unidentified man, who is believed to also be with him in Paris." It showed a grainy image of Cronin.

Alec growled. "Fuck."

"It is believed these two men, along with these other assailants"—the screen showed grainy images of Eiji, Jacques, Kennard and even Kole—"are involved with the desecration of the two hundred year old gargoyle statues on Notre Dame and numerous others around Paris."

Eiji growled at the screen. "They have evidence of a huge gargoyle that has come to life and tries to kill people, yet they're more concerned with the fact Alec turned it to dust? What is wrong with the world today?"

"The media will twist a story for what sells," Alec sat flatly.

Then a man appeared on screen. He looked homeless: disheveled, unclean, with wild eyes. "Those men saved us all," he said in French. "I saw them. That creature broke from the wall. It came to life and breathed fire. I saw it! Then the men appeared—" He opened his hands like a flash going off. "—and the creature turned on them. Then in a blink it was all gone!" The man looked insane. He sounded even more so. "I'm not the only one who saw it. There were others!"

"I thought I got them all. I thought I erased the lycan from their memories. I must have missed some...." Alec sighed deeply. "I failed to keep us secret."

Cronin pulled Alec by the arm so he would face him. "No, m'cridhe. You saved those people. And countless others. What you did was damage control. You did not set these creatures free for them to wreak havoc. You were trying to stop it."

Alec looked to the floor and his shoulders sagged. "I'm still responsible. Because of me your faces are now plastered on every wanted list. How long do you think it will be before the police, the FBI, CIA, or NSA find this place? They'll track your records, freeze your accounts." He ran his hand through his hair. "I should have known better."

"It is only money," Cronin replied. "And material things. They're of little importance to me."

Alec looked at Cronin then. "You can stop being so perfect now."

Eiji snorted but he had his arm around Jodis' waist. Cronin didn't need Alec's mind reading ability to see that Eiji had been worried. For his own life, for Jodis', Cronin wasn't sure, but it didn't matter. It was the sentiment that mattered. He pulled Alec against him and kissed the side of his head for the same reason.

"I will have some explaining to do at the next council meeting," Alec murmured. "When the world elders hear of this...."

"They will understand," Cronin soothed him. "You're not to blame."

Alec didn't seem convinced, but he didn't argue.

"Well, at least we know now that video surveillance doesn't see the time shift," Jodis said. "The footage stopped when time did."

Alec checked his watch. "Stopped again." He reset the time, but given no other vampires wore a watch, he asked his father. "Dad. How's your watch?"

Kole, who was now sitting on the sofa looking a little worse for wear, checked his wristwatch. He frowned and put it to his ear. "It's not working."

Cronin nodded. "Time truly did stop."

Alec went over and sat beside Kole on the sofa. "You okay, Dad?"

Kole gave him a tired smile. It wasn't even midday, yet he looked ready for sleep. "I'm okay. How 'bout you?"

"I'm fine. Worried about you," Alec said. He put his hand on his father's knee.

"You don't have to do that," Kole said. "Feels good but not necessary."

Alec chuckled. "I was trying to be discreet."

Kole laughed at that. "I've had aches and pains for years, and when you do your vampire Vicodin thing, everything goes away."

Alec grinned now. "I can make it permanent if you'd like? You don't ever have to feel an ache or pain again."

Kole sighed and patted Alec's knee. "Those aches and

pains are just my body's way of telling me to slow down, Alec. An ache every now and again reminds me that I'm alive. My mind still thinks I'm thirty, but my body reminds me I'm not. I'll be sixty in the fall. I can't be doing that leaping thing and running through the streets of Paris at night."

"I just wanted you to see some of the world, that's all," Alec said. "I'm sorry, I forgot how much leaping hurts."

"Don't apologize," Kole said. "I had fun! Except for the whole leaping thing and underground cave thing and the statues that moved thing and the huge stone dog-looking thing. But the scenery was nice."

Alec laughed despite the underlying sadness that Cronin could see so clearly. "Maybe next time, when all this is over, we can go somewhere else?"

Eleanor walked out with a cup of tea for Kole. He took it kindly, and with a groan as he got up, he excused himself. They went to the other living area, to the peace and quiet, where they often sat to play chess or talk.

Are you well, m'cridhe? Cronin thought directly to Alec, knowing he would hear him.

Alec's eyes shot to Cronin's. He gave a small nod. "Yeah."

Cronin hated that Alec was struggling with his father. He seemed to be holding the grains of sand of his life in his hands, only to watch helplessly as they slipped through his fingers. The harder he tried to hold on, the more impossible it was to hold.

So Cronin told him the only thing that seemed right. *You are loved, m'cridhe.*

Alec smiled a little shyly, looking down at his shirt. Oblivious to their private conversation on the other side of the room, Jacques asked, "Why Paris?"

Kennard opened his mouth. "Well, where shall I start..." but Jacques shot him a glare. Alec laughed, obviously hearing the snide mental comments from them both.

"No," Jacques started again, "why Paris exactly? Why were there so many gargoyles in Paris? From all my studies, from my time living there, I know of nothing."

Eiji frowned and turned to Jodis. "Where are there more concentrations of gargoyles?"

"France, Spain," she replied. "Mostly Europe. There was evidence of many in Russia, but they've been destroyed. There are many the world over, though they mostly are, for all intents and purposes, simply stone statues."

Alec frowned for a moment, thinking deeply. Then he looked up and Cronin knew he'd come up with something. There was a light in his eyes, a spark. "Circles. Not just my dream of the circular stone room but also the Callanish Stones. Where I was changed. And remember at the Göbekli pit," he said. "There were circles. Lots of them. We questioned their significance, their mathematical relevance, yes?" He didn't wait for anyone to answer. He went to a laptop and his fingers quickly skimmed the keyboard. He turned the laptop around so he could show everyone. On the screen was a map. "This is Notre Dame. Here is the museum where the big gargoyle was," he pointed to the screen. Then he zoomed the image out. "And this is Paris."

"Well, shit," Eiji said.

"Of course!" Jodis said.

And there on the screen was a very obvious circle. Notre Dame was at the middle of a circle of roads; Paris itself, from a distance, looked like a circle. Alec grinned. "All of Paris looks like a freakin' bull's-eye."

"Oh," Jacques mumbled. "Well, that doesn't bode well."

"And this is why there are gargoyles in Paris?" Kennard asked.

"Not just gargoyles. But Zoan activity. The Zoan used a stone circle as a portal, yes?" Alec clarified. "Well, Paris is one very big stone circle."

"So, it's more of an open portal?" Jacques asked.

Alec shook his head. "No, not any more. I think it was or might have been, but it's not anymore." Then his brow furrowed. "Those gargoyles that were on Notre Dame, when were they added? They weren't original from the twelfth century, were they?"

Jacques shook his head. "No, they were added in the eighteenth century."

"So what happened in Paris in the eighteenth century?" Alec asked, though he knew the answer. Everyone did.

The French revolution.

"Something happened with the Zoan in the French revolution," Jodis finished.

Kennard hissed. "Napoleon."

Cronin couldn't deny it wasn't possible. Napoleon rose to incredible power in a very short amount of time. His influence over the public and other politicians surely could have been the work of a vampire with the power to influence decisions and will. Napoleon might not have been a vampire himself, but maybe he had the help of one. Maybe he did have some not-so-human help in rising to power.

"The revolution was before my time," Jacques said. "But the Parisian coven elders have not mentioned any such thing."

Cronin watched as Alec closed his eyes. His eyes twitched as though he was searching his mind for something before opening. "I think we really need to speak to Gautier face-to-face," Alec said. "He's hiding something in his memory. It's well guarded, but I can see it."

"He knows about the Zoan gargoyles on Notre Dame?" Jacques asked.

Alec gave a nod. "He helped put them there."

Kennard hissed. "I knew I never liked him."

"I spoke to Gautier earlier," Jodis offered. "I phoned him in regards to the elders' meeting and briefly explained Alec's encounter with the Zoan. He never mentioned anything." Then Jodis turned around the laptop she'd been tapping away at. "But, uh, there's something else. I did a search on cities with gargoyles and circular designed arenas, landmarks, places of worship, such as the Thalos of Delphi circle in Greece, the Pantheon, or even the Colosseum. But I concentrated on churches, given the relevance to the pictograms in stained glass windows and the crypts. Notre Dame in Paris isn't the only one," she said. "There is one more." She turned the laptop around to show the screen.

There on screen was a city built in a circular formation, a city famous for its history and stone architecture, amongst other things. Cronin said the name out loud. "Rome."

"Not just Rome," Jodis replied. "Look at what is in the center of the circle."

The Vatican.

"Holy shit," Alec mumbled.

Kennard snorted. "Exactly."

Eiji laughed at that. "Well, this changes things."

"Yes, it does," Alec said. He took Cronin's hand and met his dark and determined stare. "Paris to see Gautier first? Or Rome?"

"Paris first," Cronin said. "Let's see what Gautier has to say before we tell our Italian friends we think their religious capital is the next Zoan portal."

Kennard rubbed his hands together. "Well, what are we waiting for? Let's pay Gautier a little visit."

Alec grinned at him. "We're not starting World War III, okay?"

"Of course not," he replied. "But if you'd like to magically produce the flag of England, I wouldn't mind. You know," he said with a smirk, "just as a parting gift."

Alec turned to Jodis. "Can you please let the world elders know a video conference might be in order? The sooner the better. But as for Gautier, I think the element of surprise might serve us best."

CHAPTER ELEVEN

ASIDE FROM THE unscheduled visit in his grand and ornate great-room, and being greatly outnumbered, Gautier wasn't too pleased to see them. He was startled at their very sudden appearance and yelled angrily, "What do you think you're doing here?"

Alec didn't care for niceties. He did acknowledge the other two elders in the room with a nod, but he turned and aimed his ire at Gautier. His talent of seeing the truth, seeing what Gautier was hiding, made him angry. "When Jodis called you about the elders' meeting, you withheld information. Tell us what you know."

"Don't you think you've caused enough damage?" Gautier spat. "My city is in disarray because of you."

Cronin hissed and leapt an inch from Gautier's face. "You do not speak to him that way."

Gautier took a reflexive step backward but was still defiant. "Of course you would side with him!" Then Gautier eyed Jacques. "And you! A traitor to your people!"

"Enough!" Alec yelled, and Gautier found himself physically restrained to the wall at the far side of the room by no more than Alec's glare. He kicked his legs, his feet not finding the floor, his arms pinned to the wall at his sides. "Cronin is not biased, no more than Jacques is a traitor. We came here seeking answers, which I could just rip from your mind, but I showed you the courtesy of asking. So I will repeat myself—tell us what you know. Those Zoan creatures have been here before."

Gautier nodded. His eyes were bulging, and Alec could feel the fear rolling off him. He slowly allowed Gautier's feet to slide to the floor and released his hold on him. But Alec quickly followed with another warning. "Cronin and Jacques are with me, and you will do well to remember that. Insult them again, and it will be the last thing you do."

Gautier stared at Alec, trying to sway the other two French elders to his side. His voice trembled when he spoke. "So you are the great and holy key, the one who will save us all? You make these threats, you govern over us. But who governs over you?"

Kennard let out a small laugh, and Alec could see in his mind that he was hoping Alec could turn Gautier into a squealing pig that burst into flames when he ran into sunlight. Alec turned to Kennard. "Nice thought, but he asks a fair question." Then he turned back to Gautier. "I am governed by a selected council from around the world. One I do not elect."

"And how convenient that you can influence their minds," Gautier sneered.

"Are you questioning my integrity?" Alec asked, keeping a lid on his emotions. "Then please, by all means, lodge an official complaint to the council, put in a vote of no confidence. And while you're at it, you can explain to them why you kept secret the real reason those gargoyles sat on every wall of Notre Dame. And more importantly, why you sat silent when we asked if you knew anything of the Zoan."

Gautier paled. "You can't prove anything."

"I can see it in your mind, and I could show everyone in the fucking world if I wanted to," Alec grated out. Fire and rage now licked at his words. "Napoleon knew Paris was a portal, just like Rome. He'd seen the Zoan come from the depths of the crypts underneath the cathedral, and he wanted to control them. He had a vampire adviser, didn't he? One with the talent to influence. They thought she would be able to influence the Zoan, to control them, but they killed her. And you took her role as coven leader, didn't you?"

"Lies! All lies!" Gautier shook his head incredulously, then he laughed like a madman. "Like Rome? You don't know anything!"

Cronin leapt in front of Gautier and grabbed him by the throat. "How did you overcome the Zoan? In the Revolution, how did you beat them?"

Alec put his hand to Cronin's shoulder. "Leave him. I saw in his mind how he did it." Alec glanced at the other French vampires and gave them a nod. "Let his coven decide his fate. He's been lying to you all for centuries. And Corrina?" Alec addressed the woman elder. "You wanted to know who stole your mother's Fabergé brooch. It was him. He has a vault in the Comptoir National d'Escompte de Paris, a bank founded in the revolution. Coincidence? I think not. There are deeds, jewels, art, and bonds, which he has stolen and kept secret from you all for decades. Ask him to show you."

Alec turned to see the other French coven elders staring at a scared-looking Gautier. He shook his head as they circled him, but without another glance, Alec leapt, taking everyone but the French coven with him, the sounds of Gautier's futile pleading still ringing in his ears.

ALEC PICTURED the room of the Italian coven leaders that he'd been in before and landed them all in front of the Italian elders. Benito and Viviana were, oddly enough, real life twin brother and sister. Both had been changed into vampires when the Yersinian coven wreaked havoc over much of Europe in the fourteenth century. Also known as the Black Plague, the Yersinian's wiped out one third of Italy's entire population, both human and vampire.

No older than twenty in human years, Benito and Viviana had been changed at the same time by the same Yersinian vampire trying to create his own battalion in an already losing army. As the story went, Benito and Viviana killed their maker and eventually went on to take the role of Elders. They reigned a peaceful 670 years. They were quiet and unassuming, modest yet powerful and strong. They also had connections in the very highest of places.

They were pleased Alec had been born into this vampire life as the key, happy the chosen one had a good heart. "Alec." Viviana greeted him warmly with a kiss to both cheeks. "How nice to see you again."

Benito greeted him in the same manner, then everyone else as well. Knowing Alec could read his mind didn't deter him from addressing everyone in the room. "Jodis explained your concern when she called," he said. "And as such, we have taken the liberty to make some calls of our own." He looked directly at Alec then. "I hope you do not mind?"

Alec saw directly into his mind and smiled. "Not at all. In fact, I'm grateful. And a little awestruck."

Viviana smiled proudly, pleased to honor Alec in such a way. "We are expected, so if you please...." She waved her hand.

Alec saw in her mind where they were to go, and with a mere thought, he took them all.

The floor was paved with old stone tiles, the walls a mix of Roman brick and mud, the ceiling raked with load bearing beams, and the air smelled of earth and damp. They were deep underground, and not that vampires needed light, but the only source of illumination came from a man standing near the far wall holding a lantern with a rucksack at his feet. Though he wasn't just a man. He was a priest.

He wore a white alb and a white stole with a gold cross at each end. But his zucchetto, or skullcap, was black, which told Alec this man wasn't an ordinary priest. He was a priest of the Vatican.

He raised his chin defiantly, and even though Alec could taste the man's fear of being in a room with seven vampires, he never showed it. The priest knew exactly what they were, yet he never faltered. He looked directly at Benito and Viviana and spoke in hushed Italian. "So, it is true."

Benito nodded. "Thank you for meeting with us."

Viviana opened her hand toward Alec. "Your Eminence, I introduce Ailig McAidan. The key, defender of mankind."

Well, shit. Alec wasn't sure on how to respond to that. "Um...."

The Cardinal bowed his head slightly. He spoke in English, though his accent was very thick. "It is an honor. Though I wish it were not in my lifetime." He looked up quickly and stammered to correct himself. "N-n-no offense is meant. I only wish it were not so."

Alec could see in the man's mind what he meant. Alec smiled at him and spoke directly into his mind. *I understand. I wish it weren't so either. I too wish for a life of peace.*

The priest blanched and he took a small step backwards, clearly shocked at having Alec speak to him telepathically.

So Alec looked around the small room. He knew there were tunnels and catacombs under all of Rome, and given the priest's stammering heartbeat, he thought it best to change the subject. "Where are we exactly?"

The priest swallowed hard and blinked to compose himself. "You are familiar with the Vatican Scavi?"

Alec nodded. "The Vatican Necropolis or the Tomb of St Peter, as it is also called."

The priest nodded again. "We are underneath that. The public," then he looked at the seven vampires and corrected, "*humans* do not know this place exists."

"What is it exactly?" Cronin asked.

The priest's eyes narrowed and the flickering of the lantern cast eerie shadows across his face. "These tunnels lead to the *circulus inferni*."

"The circle of hell?" Alec asked. "Oh good, because that doesn't sound ominous." He knew if the name was in Latin, then the place was *old*. And that didn't bode well.

The priest nodded seriously, missing Alec's sarcasm all together. "*Novem tibi orbibus*."

"Nine circles," Alec whispered. He certainly wasn't joking now.

"Like the nine circles of hell as depicted by Dante," Kennard added.

"It has been called many things," the priest replied.

Alec shook his head. "More like the Göbekli Tepe pits that the Zoan came through."

The priest paled at the mention of their name. "Exactly. Except these nine pits are buried deep underground here, founded by Romulus and Remus."

"The founders of Rome. Twin brothers raised by a *wolf*," Jacques murmured, shaking his head in disbelief. Alec could see the pieces of the lycan/circular portal puzzle connecting in his mind.

"A wolf?" Alec asked. "Or a lycan?"

The priest hissed. "Three thousand years ago they built the foundations of Rome to welcome the cursed creatures. Those creatures, be they called Zoan or a Biblic seraphim, rose through the pits directly from hell and were set free to roam the earth.

"It is said that Remus tried to stop Romulus from opening the portal, and Romulus killed him in return. Rome was fought over and conquered many times," the priest continued. "All for control of these pits."

"The church finally assumed control in the fourth century," Benito said with a smile. He nodded to the priest. "And they have been the keepers of them ever since."

"There's been not a murmur from these depths since that time," the priest said. "Though we knew the time of the key would come again."

"The Catholic church knows about the key?" Alec asked incredulously.

"Not just the Catholic," the priest amended. "But all dominions of faith. They each have their teachings of the key."

Cronin shook his head, disbelievingly. "The Vatican, St Peter's Basilica was built atop the pits of evil?"

The priest nodded. "Matthew 18:16. And I tell you, you are Peter, and on this rock I will build my church, and the gates of hell shall not prevail against it."

"Oh wait," Alec said, biting back a sarcastic laugh. "I've seen this movie. With the Priory of Sion and Tom Hanks. It was pretty good."

The priest gave him a scathing glare but schooled his features when he remembered just what Alec was. *The key. The one who will defeat the Zoan forever. His true purpose....*

"What is my true purpose?" Alec asked. "You just thought those words. 'His true purpose.' What does that mean?"

The priest bowed his head in apology. "To close the last portal. To rid the world of the Zoan forever."

Alec looked at the other vampires. "Wasn't my purpose to kill Queen Keket in Egypt, or Rilind in China?" He turned back to the priest. "Wasn't it?"

The priest glanced nervously at everyone. "Our prophet says the key will be born to end the unholy terror. The seraphim which flew and breathed fire shall be abolished for an eternity by he who holds the key."

"I'm pretty sure that's not in the Bible," Alec countered.

The priest smiled. "As I am certain your kind is not either, yet here you stand. There is phrasing in scriptures if one knows what to look for, Ailig. But what we've learned of this day is only granted to the initiated by telling only. It is not common knowledge, even to many in the Vatican."

"So, there is a higher order of priests who have been handed down information for thousands of years," Alec clarified, "in relation to these creatures?"

The priest nodded. "Yes."

Alec couldn't believe what he was hearing. "Hmm, I'm thinking Dan Brown was onto something."

Just then, the priest's lantern flickered and snuffed out. His heart rate took off and he sucked back a gasp. Being the only human in an underground tunnel full of vampires probably wasn't good for his heart.

Alec snapped his fingers and produced a small flame on the palm of his hand, lighting the narrow room.

Despite his fear and shock, the priest was in awe. "There is an altar to St. Erasmus in the north transept of the Basilica," he breathed. "Above our very heads."

Alec put his hand to the lantern and let the flame creep inside. "Not sure if it's St. Elmo's fire or not, but I can do a whole range of party tricks."

The priest blinked a few times, not sure of Alec's joke before he reached quickly into his rucksack. He pulled out a wooden cross and handed it to Alec. "For your protection."

Eiji snorted. "I don't think fire breathing lycan will care much for crosses."

"It's to stab them with," Alec said. "I saw it in Gautier's mind. That's how he killed a lot of the Zoan in Paris. There was a mason who turned the rest to stone, but if you hold the cross like a sword and pierce their chests, it will kill them."

Eiji grinned. "I like the sound of that."

The priest handed out crosses, though Alec handed his to Eiji. He slung his two new weapons into his thigh holsters, John Wayne style. He looked at the priest and grinned. "Are you coming with us?"

"I will wait here," the priest said. He walked to a narrow slit in the far wall and extended his hand to it. "The way down is through here. I will pray for your safe return."

Benito took the priest's hand and kissed his knuckles, then Viviana did the same. Jacques went through next, followed by Kennard, and when it was Cronin's turn, he stopped. He bowed his head to the priest, which surprised Alec.

The priest paused for a moment, then put his hand on Cronin's head and drew the sign of the cross with his thumb. "May the Lord be your strength and your shield."

Cronin replied with a soft, "*Tapadh leibh.*"

Thank you.

Alec gave the priest a nod as he passed through the small entrance, but was quick to take Cronin's hand. The earthen corridor was very narrow—like a wormhole—and there was a darkness so black that if he were still human, he wouldn't have been able to see his hand in front of his face. Eiji followed them through, and they'd gone no more than a few feet with the priest called out behind them.

"Wait!" The priest squeezed through the crack in the wall and ran to them. His swinging lantern cast waves of light through the corridor. "Wait! I will come with you."

Alec could feel the fear rolling off the priest. But the idea of willingly walking into the pits of demons with a band of vampires was abhorrently terrifying for him, yet staying behind seemed so much worse.

"Are you okay?" Eiji asked him.

The priest nodded, sweat beaded at his brow, and he held the lantern in front of him like it would protect him. He was paler still, his eyes were wide, and his heartbeat was staccato. Alec saw the man's faith and courage were mutually inclusive of the other and that was fine with him. Alec respected people who found resolve, despite their fear. It didn't matter where it came from. He looked at Eiji, who was grinning at him, and the priest balked. Alec clapped his hand on the priest's shoulder and chuckled. "Stay behind me. Eiji here might have a creepy smile, but he has our backs. You're safe with us."

Eiji laughed and the priest exhaled noisily. His breathing and shuffling feet were incredibly loud compared to the almost silent vampires. "The corridor is long," he whispered. "A few hundred feet down."

"Let's keep moving," Viviana urged them.

The descent was steep in some areas, flatter in others. The corridor curved around and narrowed in parts. Cronin walked in front with Alec close behind, and it made for awkward going, considering Alec never dropped Cronin's hand. After they'd gone a while, Alec gave Cronin's hand a squeeze. *You okay, Cronin?* He asked in his mind. He replayed the memory of him bowing his head for a blessing from the priest.

Cronin gave an embarrassed glance back at him. *It's been many a year since I have been in the company of a religious man.*

I can feel the peace it gives you, Alec told him. *Don't be embarrassed to admit these things to me.*

Is it not ridiculous? After all these years to rekindle some kind of belief? Cronin shook his head as they walked.

Not at all, Alec told him. The truth was, Alec had never paid much mind to organized religion. He wasn't brought up that way, but he had a great deal of respect for those who sought and found comfort in their faith. It was seeing the afterlife through Jorge that restored Cronin's long-lost religious beliefs. Coming from the eighth century Scotland, his faith was more Christian than Pagan, but he had disregarded his religious human life when he became vampire. Alec hadn't realized how much it had meant to him. *I'm sorry I didn't take more time to talk with you about this when you mentioned the afterlife before,* he told him.

Cronin looked back over his shoulder at Alec and gave him a smile. *Don't you see? Not only do we get this life together, but the one after it as well. I get you forever, no matter which life.*

Alec squeezed his hand again. *Two lots of eternity still won't be enough time with you.*

It is the same for me, m'cridhe.

"Alec," Benito whispered. "There is an opening ahead."

Alec threw out a protective shield around them all, though he knew it was pointless. It wouldn't stop the Zoan, but he did it anyway.

There was nothing here.

As they walked into the cavernous room, Alec cast light out to all corners. Small balls of lumen floated near the walls of earth, illuminating what was a series of interconnecting circular pits carved into the dirt and stone. Nine circular pits to be exact. But nothing moved, nothing stirred or scurried. Nothing.

Each pit had nine pillars of stone at the circumference. Each monolith had a carving of a wolf or a winged dragon-like creature. They were definitely in the right place, but it would seem, at the wrong time.

Alec easily jumped a dozen or so feet into the largest pit. "There's nothing here," Alec said. He raked his hand into the dry soil at his feet and let the grains fall through his fingers. "Not even bugs or worms will inhabit this place."

"This place is long abandoned," Kennard said, tracing his fingers along one of the carved stone pillars.

Eiji sheathed his cross into his thigh holster, disappointed. He turned to the priest. "How long ago was this abandoned?"

"Before the church assumed ownership of these lands," the priest said, scanning the large cavernous space. "According to our teachings, Romulus used these pits to summon demons from the deep, that he even gave offerings of thirty women from a neighboring town to these creatures. Though it wasn't enough to please them, and it was here they killed him. A storm of lightning and whirlwinds came through and carried him away," the priest looked up at the ceiling of dirt. "Though I don't know how that is possible."

"Believe me," Alec said. "Nothing is impossible."

The priest nodded solemnly. "It was said the storm closed the portal and took Romulus with it. Though we knew it would reopen one day when the key was born."

"If my true purpose is to close the last portal and this one has been closed," Alec wondered out loud, "then where is the portal I'm supposed to close?"

The priest shook his head slowly. "I do not know. There are many churches built over pits like this one...."

"There are what?" Alec snapped. His tone was sharp and a surge of anger rolled like thunder from him.

The priest stumbled backward. His fear was quickly quelled by his willingness to be with his God.

Alec put his hands out, sending out a bloom of calm. "I won't hurt you, but we have wasted time. Tell us what you know!"

The priest shook his head. "I've told you all I know! I don't know what the nine circles mean. There are nine circles in all facets of religions, mathematics, science. It is uncanny how many times nine circles appear...." The priest had images flash through his mind of drawings, old drawings.

"What are those?" Alec demanded. "Those drawings in your mind. I want to see them."

The priest put his hands to his head and squinted his eyes, not wanting to hide anything from Alec, but clearly not coping with the pressure. "We have drawings in our chambers. But they don't make sense. Well, not to us."

"Show me which room they are in," Alec said, jumping

out of the pit. He saw the room the priest pictured in his mind, and in the blink of an eye, he leapt them all into it.

IT WASN'T a room so much more than it was a vault. Still underground, the room was windowless and the door, a small, heavy wooden rectangle, was the only break from the huge stone blocks that made up the walls, floor, and ceiling. Along two walls, there were rows and rows of wooden drawers that reminded Alec of spice drawers in Chinese herbal shops and along the third wall, a large wooden desk.

The priest sucked back a scream as they arrived, the aftershocks of leaping still fraying his nerves. The shaking lantern in his hand had snuffed out. Alec sent up a ball of lumen so the priest wasn't enclosed in complete darkness. It took him a second to get his bearings, and the loud banging on the door spurred him into a flurry of action.

"Who is in there?" a man's voice bellowed in Italian. Then there was a jingling of keys.

"It is Archbishop Gänsen," the priest said, his voice shaking. "I insist all is fine and that you leave me be."

There was the persistent rattle of keys as the assailant tried several in the lock. "How did you get in there?"

"I said leave me be!" Gänsen yelled. He hurriedly opened several of the small square drawers, muttering to himself until he found what he was after. He carefully pulled out a small book bound in crumbling leather. He took a deep breath and turned to face the seven vampires who were watching him. He handed the book to Alec with shaking hands. "Here it is."

"Let me guess," Alec said, as he gently flicked through

the coarse but delicate paper, seeing drawings and scripts in calligraphy. "Leonardo Da Vinci."

Gänsen shook his head. "These were drawn by Peter himself."

"*Saint* Peter?" Alec asked, unable to hide his shock.

Gänsen nodded. "They are very old."

Alec couldn't argue that. "Here," he said, finding a page of interest. He put it on the table so everyone could see it. "Novem tibi orbibus."

There, drawn in scratchy faded ink, were the nine interconnecting circular pits they'd just visited buried deep under where they now stood. But there were lines drawn through them, intersecting angles and numbers and what appeared to be dates written along them.

"What are these dates?" Alec asked.

Gänsen shook his head. "We don't know. We thought they may mean a return of the demons, but the dates have passed throughout history without incident."

Then Viviana thought something that turned Alec's head. "What do you mean?" he asked her.

She smiled at him. "They're not dates. They're planetary projections. I study astronomy, and these"—she traced her finger along two of the lines—"are the courses of the equinoxes for Jupiter and Mars."

Alec saw a slideshow scroll through her mind that looked like a NASA equation of putting man on the moon. He stored the information in his memory for later interpretation, if he could even begin to understand it, just as the small door burst open behind them.

Two priests entered the room and recoiled when they saw who was inside, both taking a reflexive step backward. One recited a Latin prayer to repel Satan and the other drew the sign of the cross on his own forehead.

"I told you to leave me be!" Gänsen roared at them.

Alec waved his hand at the two priests and they went completely slack where they stood. Their arms lowered to their sides. Their faces went blank.

Gänsen's gaze went from the two men to Alec. "What did you do to them?"

"They're fine," Alec said. "Completely unharmed, awake, just very docile."

Gänsen put his hand to his forehead and shook his head, as though he literally couldn't believe what he was in the middle of. Alec redirected the conversation back to the book. "You said these drawings didn't make sense?"

Gänsen turned to the next page. "We don't know what this is."

On the next page were the circles again, with the lines drawn through them as on the previous page. Only this time, from each point where a line crossed the circumference of a circle, another line came off it to meet in the center. There were nine lines, meeting at a central point.

"Oh wow," Viviana said.

Cronin shot a glance to Alec and smiled. "It's a nine-point circle."

"A what?" Gänsen asked.

"A nine-point circle," Alec repeated softly. "Wow, indeed. Saint Peter was onto them. He knew how to do this almost two thousand years before mathematicians. This is incredible."

Gänsen shook his head. "I don't follow."

Cronin explained. "These circles are the formation of the pits. The center circle is the important one, the largest. Each surrounding circle cuts through the main circle at a certain point, and these lines give us a triangle, or in this case, a pyramid."

Eiji said, "The Göbekli Tepe pits are of the same configuration. The nine-point circle and the subsequent pyramid the shape makes is ground zero."

"It is a geometrical marvel," Benito said, "that Saint Peter was able to do this in his time."

Gänsen turned the next page. "But he didn't understand it." And there on a third drawing was the nine circles, the triangle, and scratches of frustration through the whole diagram. Saint Peter himself had furiously crossed out several attempts at trying to figure it out.

Viviana smiled. "Because these lines depict the celestial paths of the planets," she said simply. "Saint Peter wouldn't have understood the significance because he lived in a time when planets had not been discovered."

Alec nodded. It was all coming together. "So when the nine planets make this formation"—he turned the page back to the drawing of the nine circles—"the triangle it makes will form an inverted pyramid, of sorts. And that is what opens the portal."

Alec pictured the image in his mind and shared it with those around him. Better than any computer image or hologram, he could picture the planets in formation and the lines through their axes would form the upside down pyramid toward earth. "Does that look right?" he asked Viviana, and she nodded.

Gänsen blinked several times. "What was that?"

"Telepathic projection," Alec answered. "Sorry. It's just easier than trying to explain."

The priest gawped at him. "How do you do those magic tricks?"

Alec shrugged one shoulder. "We don't know really. I have many gifts. Most are unexplainable. It's not magic though, and they're not really gifts either. I'd give them back if they were."

That got him a few glances from the vampires around him, as though they could not believe he'd say such a thing. Cronin put his hand to Alec's back, knowing all too well that out of everything being the key gave Alec, all he really wanted was a sense of normalcy.

"We must go home, m'cridhe," Cronin said softly.

"Agreed." Alec looked at his friends. "Benito, Viviana, would you please come with us to New York? I can bring you back to Rome whenever you'd like, but I might need your help, Viviana, working out planetary stuff."

She bowed her head. "It would be an honor." Then she eyed the book on the table. "We may need that."

Gänsen started to object, but Alec put out his hand and picked up the ancient book. "No, the original stays here. It is only right," Alec said, and Gänsen sagged with relief. "But I could take a copy," Alec said. He held the book in one hand and made a replica appear in his other.

Gänsen's mouth fell open, and Alec handed him the original. "I have the talent of replication or duplication," he explained with a shrug. "Some talents have their perks."

Alec turned and asked if everyone was ready, but Eiji said, "Ah, Alec." He nodded to the two docile priests still staring blankly into space.

"Oh." Alec nodded in their direction and they both startled back to normal. Alec looked right at them and pointed to Gänsen. "This man should be commended for his bravery and for his commitment to God. He helped save the world today."

Then with no more than a thought, he left the three priests alone in the dungeon room and leapt everyone back to the apartment in New York.

CHAPTER TWELVE

WITH JUST AN HOUR or so before the coven meeting, Alec explained everything they'd found out and showed them a telepathic slideshow of where they'd been and what they'd seen. Including the encounter with Gautier, to which no one seemed too surprised. And he showed them Saint Peter's book he had duplicated from the Vatican.

Jodis took the book, like it wasn't a replica, with two careful hands and a wondrous smile. "Oh, Alec," she cooed.

Pretending to be offended, Eiji put out both hands. "And what am I? Did you not miss me at all?"

Jodis quickly threw her arms around him, and he lifted her and twirled her around, making her laugh. Then she gasped. "Be careful of the book, my love."

Eiji set her back on her own two feet and kissed the side of her head with smiling lips. Jodis, speaking fluent Italian, greeted Benito and Viviana with warm kisses to their cheeks, saying it had been far too long since they'd seen each other. They soon had the replica book open on the table, along with notepads and pens and laptops, and were in deep conversation about planets and nine-point circles.

Alec barely had time to think. With a deep sigh, he walked into his and Cronin's walk-in closet to change his clothes. With a clean shirt on, he pulled up his jeans and was doing up his fly when familiar hands cupped his face. *Cronin.* The mere thought of Cronin, the close proximity, calmed him, centered him. He closed his eyes and leaned his face into Cronin's palms and sighed again.

Cronin's soft voice whispered in Alec's mind. *You never rest.*

Alec agreed with a nod. *I never have alone time with you. It's all I want. Just peace and quiet, and you.*

Cronin smiled. "As do I, m'cridhe." He ghosted his lips to Alec's, just as there was a knock on their bedroom door.

"It's time," Eiji called. "We can't be late, brothers."

Alec sighed. He stole a quick kiss from Cronin and said, "Come on. Let's get this over with."

He took Cronin's hand and led him back out to the living room. Once a peaceful sanctuary where they could lounge on the sofa, cuddle, and talk, it was now a bustling hive of activity.

Eiji put his hand to Jodis' shoulder, where she and Viviana were still furiously working out planetary alignments, paths, and dates. "Are you ready, my love?"

She looked up at him and smiled. "I cannot go."

Eiji's face fell. "Oh."

"My sweetest Eiji," she said, putting her hand to his face. "We are so close to figuring this out," she said. "I can't be in two places at once."

"I understand," he whispered.

She kissed him softly. "I promise when all this is over, you and I will spend a decade in Japan. Just us."

He smiled and gave her a nod. "I will hold you to that."

She kissed him again, this time with smiling lips, and

turned back to join Viviana in working out improbable mathematic equations. Alec hated that his responsibilities were weighing his friends down as well. For vampires who would live an eternity, they sure were always short on time.

Alec looked at Cronin and smiled. He closed off his mind and concentrated, and with all the power he could summon, he let one word scream through his mind.

Stop!

And time stopped.

Everyone in the room stopped, frozen in time, except for Cronin, who still held Alec's hand. "Alec? Is something wrong?"

Alec smiled at him and kissed him. "Yes. We're out of time. All I wanted was a moment with you, and then I remembered that was something I could have." He kissed Cronin again, but before Cronin could deepen it, Alec pulled back. "And not just us."

He walked over to the table and touched Jodis' arm. She startled to life, taking in the frozen room around her. She saw Cronin but looked back at Alec. "What's wrong?"

"I stopped time," he said. "Just for us."

"How?" she asked. "Can you control it better?"

Alec laughed quietly. "I don't know. Maybe it doesn't freeze who I want it to at that time? I really don't know. Jodis, right now it doesn't matter how my talents work. See this man here?" Alec nodded to Eiji, who was standing frozen in time. His long black hair was pulled back, a few wisps feathered down, and his eyes were fixed on where Jodis had been. "He loves you more than I can explain. He needs you. I know you're busy, we all are, and I am eternally grateful for your help and dedication. But he needs a few moments with you. Just you."

Jodis' eyes welled with tears. "Oh."

Then Alec put his hand on Eiji's arm, breaking the hold time had on him. Eiji spun, startled, and drew a wooden cross in each hand from his thigh holsters. "Where...?" Then seeing they were alone and everyone else was still frozen in time, he straightened. "What happened?"

Jodis smiled at him. "Everything's fine," she said. She took the wooden crosses out of his hands, and standing close against him, she slid them back into his thigh holsters. Eiji's pupils dilated, and she whispered against his lips, "Alec has given us the gift of time. I suggest we use it wisely."

Eiji grinned, snatched up Jodis' hand, and led her toward their bedroom. He never said a word, but the next sound Alec heard was their door closing and Jodis' laughter.

Cronin walked slowly over to Alec. "You are a good man."

In the blink of an eye, Alec had Cronin on his back in the middle of their bed and was firmly between his thighs. He ghosted a kiss over Cronin's mouth. "I'm not a man," he said, flexing his vampire fangs. He turned Cronin's head, exposing his neck, and sank his teeth into his flesh.

Cronin bucked, grinding his hips into Alec's, and with both hands on Alec's ass, he pulled him closer. Alec moaned as the sweet taste of Cronin filled his mouth and slid down his throat.

Oh Alec, I need you closer still. Your teeth... your skin... your body... you inside me.... Cronin's thoughts were a jumbled mess, swirling with desire and need.

Alec fisted Cronin's shirt and ripped it open, exposing his chest. He pulled back, only long enough to undo his jeans and pull them from his body. He leaned down and planted a soft kiss to the scar on Cronin's chest, and Cronin roughly dragged Alec's shirt over his head. He growled in frustration. "Alec."

Alec smiled victoriously. He loved it when Cronin was desperate; the urgency, the pure need—it rolled off him, fueling Alec's desire. Resting back on his haunches, he undid his button fly and released his hard cock from the confines of the denim. Alec leapt the lube from the drawer into his hand and smeared it over his shaft and cockhead, then added more to Cronin's ass.

Cronin snatched the lube from him and tossed it to the floor. He gripped Alec around the neck and pulled him over him. "I need you now."

"I don't want to hurt you."

Cronin answered by hitching his legs even higher and hooking his ankles behind Alec's back. He rolled his hips, desperate for Alec to fill him.

Please.

Alec pushed inside in one hard thrust, taking any pain Cronin felt and replacing it with pure ecstasy. Cronin's eyes widened and his whole body convulsed and writhed as Alec speared him with his cock.

Cronin's mind was blank, no coherent thoughts, only pleasure and bliss on every synapse, every nerve. His hard cock pressed between them, smearing precum on their stomachs. And when Alec thought it might be too much for him, Cronin held him tighter, harder.

Fuck, fuck, Cronin murmured in his mind.

Cronin rarely cursed, mentally or vocally, but Alec loved it when he rolled those words through his mind, his Scottish accent lilting the sound perfectly.

I love fucking you, Alec whispered into his mind.

Cronin gasped.

I love being inside you. Can you feel how good it feels for me? Alec asked. Then using his empathic abilities, he flooded Cronin with every sensation, every emotion he felt when they made love.

Cronin gasped loudly and arched his back as he came. He went rigid, his head thrown back, his mouth open, as his cock spilled between them.

Alec thrust harder, wringing out every ounce of pleasure from Cronin's orgasm until Cronin was a shaking, trembling mess. His body was boneless, pliable, and spent, so Alec kissed him until he moaned. Then he kissed him some more, filling his mouth with his tongue, thrusting into him as he did.

Cronin put his hands to Alec's face, cradling him as their tongues twirled and tasted. But then Cronin pulled Alec's mouth away and turned his face so he could sink his teeth into Alec's neck.

As soon as Cronin's teeth pierced Alec's skin, he came. Pleasure barreled through him as he released deep inside Cronin.

And as Cronin's mind began to come back together, the fractured remnants of pleasure still scattering coherent thought, there was one word that sounded in his mind.

How he felt when they made love, how it felt when Alec came inside him, was *home.*

Resting on his elbows, Alec put his hands to Cronin's face. "You are home to me as well."

Cronin closed his eyes, as if Alec's words were sunlight and he was bathing in the warmth. When he opened his eyes again, he asked, "Is the world still stopped out there?"

"Yes," Alec said. "Except for Eiji and Jodis—Oh God," he cringed, "I'm gonna need brain bleach after seeing that."

Cronin burst out laughing and rolled them both over so he was on top. "Sorry for making you think of them."

Alec grinned at him. "Normally I can block that out,

but you've riddled my brain with pheromones. I'm not thinking clearly."

"*I* riddled your brain with pheromones?" Cronin asked. "What on earth did *you* do to *me*? I couldn't even speak!"

Alec laughed at that. "You weren't complaining."

"Oh, I'm not complaining," he replied. Then he sighed and his smile slid away. "Any sign of the Zoan?"

Alec shook his head. "No. They're still there, though. They're just... busy."

"Busy doing what?"

"I don't know," Alec replied. "I can't see exactly... getting ready for us?"

Cronin got up and held his hand out to Alec, helping him off the bed. "We best not keep them waiting." They cleaned up a little, then Cronin walked into the closet to get new, not-ripped-to-shreds clothes, and Alec redid the buttons on his jeans. Cronin came back out to the bed and threw a shirt to Alec, which Alec pulled on over his head, and Cronin smiled at him. He gently put his hand to Alec's face. "Thank you, m'cridhe. For giving us this time, for knowing what I needed. And for giving Eiji and Jodis some time also."

"It was the least I could do for them," Alec said. "After all they do for us, for me." And right on cue, Eiji laughed from the room up the hall. It made Alec smile. "And that is a sound I'll never get tired of hearing."

Cronin kissed him softly. "*Tha gaol agam ort.*"

Alec hummed as Cronin's words settled in his heart. "I love you, too." Then he smiled. "Eiji, coming through that door in three, two, one...."

The door opened and Eiji walked in like the room was his. Without stopping, he grabbed Alec by the face and kissed both his cheeks. "God bless you," he said, then simply walked out without another word.

Jodis stood in the doorway. "Thank you, Alec."

"You're most welcome," he replied. He led Cronin by the hand and made sure everyone was in the exact positions they were in before, and with a calming breath and burst of his mental powers, the room sprang into action and noise.

"We all ready?" Alec said.

"Am now," Eiji replied with a wink. Jodis giggled, earning a strange look from Viviana.

Alec put his hand to Jodis' arm. *I'm transferring to you the power to leap. If anything happens, you get everyone out of here, okay?*

She replied with no more than a smile and nod. Alec turned to everyone else: Cronin, Eiji, Kennard, Jacques, and Benito. "Ready?"

And they were gone.

THE WAREHOUSE where the meeting was held was the same warehouse a very human Alec had come to with Cronin eighteen months ago when they had held a coven meeting in regards to information on the key. It was big enough to house the Eastern coven, some four hundred vampires that called the Eastern Seaboard area home.

When they arrived, a silence fell across the warehouse, though Alec was hit with a wave of four hundred mental voices. It took him a moment to compartmentalize the sounds and images and shut them down. "Welcome and thank you for being here," Alec said in greeting. He waved his hand at the two non-American-known vampires in his company, introducing them to everyone present. "This is

Kennard, London elder, and Benito, Roman elder. They have joined me in this latest quest, which is why I've asked you all to come tonight."

"The gargoyles in Paris," one vampire prompted.

Alec nodded. "Yes. Also known as Zoan, they are lycan-type creatures—" A hiss went through the warehouse. "—who were turned to stone gargoyles. But it's the ones that aren't stone, the living Zoan, that brings me here tonight.

"If you'll allow me to show you," Alec said warily. "I can project the images of these Zoan into your minds so you can see what they look like."

"It will look like a memory," Cronin told them. "In your mind's eye."

"Don't be alarmed," Alec added, then with a deep breath he centered himself. Using all the mental strength he could muster, he pushed out his vivid recall of the lycan creatures, half-wolf, half-dragon into the four hundred minds in front of him.

Someone gasped. "So it is true? They breathe fire?"

Alec pulled back the mental image and felt it snap like a rubber band in his mind. He shook his head, a small detail Cronin didn't miss. He looked immediately concerned. "Are you well, Alec?"

Alec nodded. "Yeah. Just took more out of me than I realized." *I've never done that to this many people, that's all. I'm fine.*

Eiji took over, and gave a very short version of what they knew. "They somehow use ancient pits as a gateway to get here. Whether that's a portal to another dimension or to another time, we don't know. But there is an energy within these circular sites, similar to how Alec was changed, that opens to allow them through."

"We think it has to do with planetary alignment," Benito added. "We're working on that now."

"We've been to London, France, Italy," Cronin said. "The stone Zoan gargoyles in Paris were active when Alec was near but nowhere else."

"How come?" one vampire asked.

Alec explained, "Some gargoyles are simply stone statues, man-made. Some, however, were Zoan that have been turned to stone. It is these creatures that are our concern."

"What does it have to do with us?" someone asked.

A few vampires didn't take kindly to that, Cronin included, but Alec was quick to answer. He put his hand up, making the warehouse quiet. "It's a fair question," he replied. "Technically speaking, it has nothing to do with you. Yet, somehow it has everything to do with you. These Zoan creatures will kill any vampire they come across. They have threatened me personally but have also shown me their intent to slaughter the human population of New York. So if you wish to be oblivious and unprepared, then feel free to leave now. I will not blame you, nor ask questions. But if you *do* leave, the blame for your families' death by the hand of Zoan will rest on no one's shoulders but your own."

The warehouse was still and quiet. No one left. Cronin smiled.

Alec took charge of the room, having the undivided attention of everyone there. He pulled out a wooden cross from the back of his jeans and held it up so everyone could see it. "A living Zoan can only be killed by one of these." A few vampires laughed and Alec smiled. He held the cross by the short top, like a small sword. "No normal wooden stake will kill them, but a wooden cross to the chest will. It is how the French killed them in the Revolution."

No one was laughing now.

"A stone gargoyle that has come to life can be killed by any means necessary," Alec explained. "Smashing it to dust would be my preferred choice."

"Are you truly expecting the Zoan to come to America?" someone else asked.

Alec took a deep breath before answering. "Yes."

A hum of whispers spread through the warehouse, then one voice from the back of the warehouse said, "Alec, Elders, I think they're already here."

Silence boomed through the warehouse, and the sea of vampires opened up to the vampire that had spoken. A pretty woman, late twenties, with dark skin and a white coat came forward. "Yvette Gates, Pennsylvania," she introduced herself with a nod. "There was a news report earlier tonight, though they called it a hoax after the gargoyles in Paris. The famous gargoyles that guard the Eastern State Penitentiary, well, they're gone."

Alec saw the news segment play through Yvette's memory. The huge stone gargoyles were indeed no longer perched at the entrance gates. The chains that tethered them to their stone pillars were snapped. Alec looked to Cronin, then to Eiji and Kennard and Benito. "It's no hoax."

"We should go there," Eiji said. He put his hands on the crosses in his thigh holsters but didn't draw them out.

Before Alec could answer him, Yvette said, "The police are calling it a hoax, but they're all over it. They're not letting on what's really happened."

"The police," Alec mumbled. His gaze shot to Cronin and he held out his hand for him to hold. Then he looked at Eiji. "We're going. But not to the penitentiary." Alec turned to the coven of vampires. "If anyone hears or sees anything, you must contact us. But please, stay aware, and be safe."

"Where are we going?" Kennard asked.

Alec smiled. "To see some old friends of mine."

THE THIRTY-THIRD PRECINCT hadn't changed at all. It was close to midnight, so some desks were empty, and given Alec had always worked the nightshift, it looked exactly the same as when he'd left it.

Which, admittedly, had left his police colleagues—and the rest of the world—reeling at the sight of two men disappearing into thin air. Having five men suddenly appear in the middle of the department floor had a similar effect.

One cop spilled his coffee down the front of himself. One threw a file into the air in shock. Most all of them took several reflexive steps back, and in the next second raised and aimed their guns at them.

Alec smiled. "Oh, the déjà vu."

In no time they were completely surrounded by NYPD. They kept their distance a safe few feet back from a room full of familiar faces, now pale and afraid. "Alec MacAidan, you are under arrest," one detective said.

Alec snorted out a laugh. "I don't think so, Patel." He waved his hand and their guns all dropped to the floor with a clatter and cries of shock from some of the officers. Alec ignored them. "Where's De Angelo?"

Some cops fumbled to pick up their weapons with shaking hands; some walked backwards in fear. Alec sneered at them, his ex-colleagues who had made fun of him for years for being the one that weird-shit happened to. "Who's laughing at who now?" he whispered.

Eiji did in fact laugh at that, and the policemen closest to Eiji all moved back a few more steps.

One of the detectives, Steinberg, who had laughed at Alec the night he told them he saw a man turn to dust in his arms, almost picked his gun up. Alec put his arm out and leapt the Glock into his own hand, making all the police officers gasp and curse in shock and fear. Alec took two long strides to where Steinberg stood, ashen and slack-jawed. Alec squeezed the Glock, mangling it in his hand, handed him the bent metal, and smiled. "De Angelo?"

The door to the captain's office flew open, and the big man appeared in the doorway. De Angelo looked the same, save the gray hair that now peppered through his hair. "MacAidan," he barked, though there was no bite in it. He looked at Cronin, Eiji, Kennard, and Benito, then back to Alec. "You've got a helluva hide coming back in here."

Alec smiled at him. "It's good to see you again too, Captain."

De Angelo's dark skin flushed from both anger and a dash of fear. He was braver than Alec gave him credit for. "You're under arrest, MacAidan. We've got footage—"

Alec cut him off with a well-aimed glare. "Yeah, yeah. Patel's already tried that line. I don't think so. We need to talk. Now."

A young and stupid cop, one Alec didn't know, made a lunge at Kennard, who was standing at the back of their group. Alec put his hand out. "You don't want to do that," Alec said, and every cop in the department froze, like deer in headlights. Alive and awake, but docile: unable and unwilling to move.

De Angelo remained unaffected and stumbled back a step. "Wh-wh-what did you do?"

"I saved them from being hurt," Alec replied. What Alec didn't say was if anyone tried to hurt any of his friends, he'd cheerfully kill them where they stood. "Captain, we need to talk about what's going on."

De Angelo nodded, and Alec could feel the captain's fear now. *Good*, Alec thought. He'd never really gotten off on the whole scary-vampire thing, but sometimes a healthy dose of fear really drove a point home.

De Angelo walked woodenly back to his desk and sat in his chair like he was expecting every breath to be his last; sweat beaded his brow. Alec sat across from him in a chair he'd sat in many times and smiled. "The gargoyles coming to life in Paris was not a hoax or an act of computer imagery. The footage of us appearing and disappearing on the street near the River Seine was as real as us appearing in the middle of the department floor a minute ago, as real as when I disappeared from here a year and a half ago."

De Angelo glanced at Cronin. *With him.*

"Yes, with him," Alec said.

De Angelo's eyes almost bugged out of his head. *He can hear my thoughts....*

"Among a good many other things," Alec said, and De Angelo's mind spun. Alec snapped his fingers, bringing De Angelo back to his senses. "The news report of the Eastern State Penitentiary...." Alec trailed off, allowing De Angelo to fill in the blanks.

"The uh, there was um." De Angelo cleared his throat. "You don't have clearance for that information."

Alec snorted. "You don't have clearance for knowing we exist, yet here we are. We're playing nice. I wanted to help, Captain," Alec said. His tone was ice cold. "Okay, so let me tell you what I know. The gargoyles at the penitentiary were not stolen. They are in fact creatures that call themselves Zoan. Think lycan. You've seen those *Underworld* movies, right?"

De Angelo nodded mechanically and swallowed hard.

"Well, kinda like that," Alec went on. "Only different. They were turned to stone and mounted at the gates as a warning. Why they came to life and broke free is the tricky part. I won't bother explaining the whole circle, portal, hole-in-the-universe theory, only that if those gargoyles came to life in Pennsylvania then chances are the same will happen here in New York. They have threatened this city. And you need to be ready for that."

De Angelo blinked, his mind was scrambling.

"The stone creatures can be killed easily enough," Alec said. "Smash 'em with a hammer if you have to. Shoot 'em. Whatever works. It's the not-stone ones you need to be careful of. They're big, dangerous, breathe fire. That kind of thing."

"Breathe fire?" De Angelo whispered.

"Yep. You following?" Alec asked. "They can also stop time." Alec wondered how he could explain that without sounding ridiculous, realized he couldn't, so he just kept going. "So, technically speaking, they can just freeze everything and you'll be none the wiser... and probably dead. In which case, this has been a waste of time. But on the off chance that they don't stop time or you do survive, you'll need to notify the entire NYPD on how to take them down."

De Angelo's brain was having trouble keeping up. Alec reasoned that it was a lot to take in, so he gave him a moment. He then put a wooden cross on De Angelo's desk. "A cross, not a stake, *a cross* speared through the chest will do it. Oh, and they're not fond of mercury."

De Angelo blinked slowly. "Uh."

"We're gonna do our best to take them out," Alec told him. "But if we fail, then you'll need to know how to keep the city safe. You should notify the boys down at Pennsylvania. There's been Zoan activity there, so they should be told as well. Then possibly the military, just to be safe."

Cronin smiled at Alec. *Once a policeman....*

Alec snorted and smiled back at him.

"What are they?" De Angelo asked. "I mean, what am I supposed to say? They'll think I'm crazy!"

Alec glared at him then. "What? Like you laughed at me when I told you what I saw?"

De Angelo paled and leaned back in his chair. He looked at the five faces staring back at him and had trouble swallowing. "Uh, about that...."

"Just do as I say," Alec said. "We've come here in good faith. You needed fair warning. Consider it given. Do with it what you will." Alec shot a look at the surveillance camera in the corner. "Show them the footage. It wouldn't be the first time CCTV footage was leaked out of this office."

De Angelo didn't even bite at that. "How will they come? Where?"

"I would hazard a guess at any of the older churches," Alec said. "Anything that's old and has gargoyles. But it could be anywhere."

Before De Angelo could reply, Eiji's cell phone buzzed in his pocket. He quickly put it to his ear, listened, and clicked off the call. He spoke so low that the human in the room couldn't hear. "That was Jodis. She says they've found something they need to show us right away."

Alec stood and Cronin was quick to stand beside him. He moved too fluidly, too quickly, so that the crystal clear thought that ran through De Angelo's mind was *What are they?*

Alec turned his stare back to De Angelo. *None of your*

concern is what we are. Then, in his mind he flashed him a fanged snarl, and De Angelo's breath left him in a whoosh as he recoiled in his chair. Alec smiled in satisfaction and spoke directly into his mind. *I've done the right thing in letting you know about this, so now it's your turn. Leave my father alone. He's an old man, and no amount of surveillance or detail on him will ever lead you to me. You understand?*

De Angelo nodded weakly.

"Oh, and one more thing," Alec said. He leaned over De Angelo's desk and put his index finger to the captain's stained, most favorite coffee cup. De Angelo's eyes almost fell out of his head as the cup before him changed into the colors of the rainbow. "Just as a reminder of who I really am. You know, still gay."

Eiji barked out a laugh, almost scaring De Angelo to death. Alec nodded toward the department floor where all the cops still stood catatonic and they burst out of their stupors. They spun looking for the intruders and someone yelled, "The Captain!" making all officers turn to face them through the window.

Before they could raise their guns, Alec smiled at De Angelo. "It's been fun."

And they were gone.

CHAPTER THIRTEEN

VIVIANA AND JODIS were waiting by the dining table along with Jacques, Kole, and Eleanor, while Adelmo and Jorge sat on the sofa reading a book. Eiji was quick to give Jodis a kiss on the cheek before sliding his arm around her waist. "What did you find, my love?"

"I think we've figured out what it all means," she said. "Well, Viviana did. See this here?" She pointed to a hand-drawn sketch. "This is the layout of the Göbekli Tepe pits in Turkey, the portal these Zoan creatures came through."

"And this," Viviana added, turning the laptop screen around so everyone could see it, "is the planetary alignments on the day you were changed, Alec."

Jodis held the hand-drawn sketch over the laptop screen. "Superimposed, they're identical."

"What does that mean?" Cronin asked.

Viviana answered. "See how the circles are situated for the portal to be open, we believe it needs to be mirrored for the portal to close. Look at Saint Peter's drawings again." She turned the book around on the table so it faced them. "See how he's mirrored it here? We assumed it was because it made no sense to him—he didn't even know what planets were."

"But you think it's something else?"

They both nodded. "We do."

"It's mirrored or reversed for a reason."

Alec saw where they were going with this. "This one, like the Göbekli Tepe pits, opened the portal," he said, pointing to the first drawing. "And the mirrored one will close it."

Jodis grinned at him and nodded. "Yes."

"So we need the planets to make the opposite formation of when Alec was changed?" Cronin asked.

"Exactly," Viviana said.

"When does that occur?" Eiji asked.

Viviana showed them a page of mathematical equations and orbital projections. "Now."

"Awesome," Alec said sarcastically. "So we have exactly no time to find the pits somewhere in the world that match this drawing?" He pointed to the second drawing by Saint Peter.

"Well, we already have," Jodis said, handing Alec an iPad. "Here." There on the screen was a floor plan of one of the world's most famous churches. She then slid the hand-drawn planetary alignment sketch Viviana had done, and it was easy to see the circular formation was one and the same.

"St. Basil's Cathedral in Moscow."

Jodis nodded then clicked on the laptop keyboard, bringing up another screen. It was an image from Google Maps of Moscow. The old city had been built in a circular formation, and if it were a target, St. Basil's was the bull's-eye.

Alec ran his hands through his hair and sighed. He was tired, weary. Something he'd not felt since he was human.

Are you well, m'cridhe? Cronin's soothing voice whispered into his mind.

It was like a warm blanket around him and it made Alec smile. *Just tired.*

Cronin frowned. *You could stop time and rest?*

Alec shook his head. *No, let's finish this.* "This is the Muscovites calling." He looked at Eiji. "We need all the weapons and supplies we have."

Eiji never questioned him, just raced out of the room. Cronin on the other hand, tilted his head. "The Muscovites?"

"The elders from Moscow," Alec explained. "On the phone."

The room was quiet for a moment, then sure enough the phone on the table buzzed. Jodis picked it up, but before she answered, Alec simply said, "Tell them we're on our way. The world elders will have to wait for a council meeting. We're out of time."

Jodis answered the call, and even though Alec could hear every word spoken, he didn't need to. *The creatures you asked about are here. They're coming out of the crypts.*

Eiji ran back into the room with the bulletproof vests they'd used before and some quivers and thigh holsters. He had a few wooden arrows and stakes in each hand, though Alec saw he was worried they had no crosses.

We'll get some there, Alec reassured him.

Without a word, Jodis picked a thigh holster and strapped it to her leg. Eiji smiled at her. "You're never so beautiful as you are when you're kicking someone's ass."

She grinned at him as she fastened the last strap. "And the same goes for you, my love."

Alec fixed the clasps to Cronin's vest and then Cronin did Alec's. It had become a bit of a tradition that they fit each other's vests and weapons before going into battle. Each man quite capable of doing his own but relished the quiet moment of love and protection it symbolized. When he was done, Alec walked over to Jacques. Alec could see the internal debate the vampire waged with himself: torn between wanting to fight alongside his coven family and wanting to protect Kole.

Alec put his hand on Jacques' arm and spoke directly into his mind. *There's no job more important to me and I know it's more than I'm entitled to ask for, but please stay and look after him.*

Of course. Jacques gave him a nod. Then he smiled. *You know you're sounding more like Cronin every day.*

He's wearing off on me. Then with a glance at Kole and Eleanor, he said, *I'm transferring leaping to you again. If you need it, get them all out of here.*

Jacques nodded. "Of course."

Then it was time to face his father. Kole looked exhausted. It was well after midnight and the dark circles under his eyes made him look even older than his years. "Dad," Alec whispered, quickly embracing him. "Get some sleep. I'll be back before you wake up."

Kole scoffed. "You know that's not gonna happen. I'll wait till I know you're back safe and sound. Then I'll sleep."

"Sounds familiar," Cronin said, now standing beside Alec.

Kole smiled at him. "Look after my boy, 'kay?"

Cronin bowed his head. "With my life."

Then Jorge ran over to Alec and jumped up into his arms. "Jorge come with you?"

Jorge's eyes were big and hopeful. His little grin made his cheeks even chubbier, but Alec shook his head. "No. You and Adelmo stay here. You're safer here."

Jorge frowned. "We can't see them. The Zoan hides from us."

"They hide from me too," Alec said.

"Alec hasn't seen them in many days," Jorge said.

"Nope. I haven't."

"Jorge doesn't like it," Jorge said. "We can't see them."

Alec looked deep into the boy's mind, into the realm of vampires long passed. He saw a swirling whisper of his mother's face and her mouth opened, though it was Jorge's voice he heard. The little boy's eyes were solid black. "We can't see them, Alec. Willem and Johan have searched for anything that may help you, but they've found nothing. If the portal is opened and Jorge is there, we may be able to guide you."

"Jorge is to come with us?"

"It may be the only way."

Alec sighed deeply, and Jorge shook his head, making the whites of his eyes reappear. The little boy beamed with happiness and excitement. "Jorge go with you!"

Alec nodded and looked to Adelmo. "I'm sorry."

He felt every ounce of the vampire-father's anguish. "I will not leave him. Where he goes, I go."

"I would never expect you to leave him," Alec told him. "I just wish there was another way."

Adelmo bowed his head. "As do I."

Kennard, Benito, and Viviana were waiting alongside Jodis and Eiji. "So we are ready?" Eiji asked. His smile was huge.

"We have no plan, no maps of what's underneath St. Basils, no visions of what will happen, no clue what to expect, and no clue what the Zoan are up to or what they're really capable of," Alec said.

Eiji grinned impossibly wider and nodded. "Like I said, we're totally ready."

Alec resisted rolling his eyes, he took a hold of Cronin's hand, and then he leapt them all to Moscow.

THE ROOM in Moscow where they landed was large and reminded Alec of a grand ballroom, only with dark timber walls and floor. Even the ceiling was dark. There were no windows at all, and although the place looked somewhat foreboding, the three vampires who stood awaiting Alec's arrival were smiling.

Alec was bombarded with a swift barrage of new mental voices and images. Though he spoke very little Russian, most of which were curse words, he could see in their minds that these coven elders were harsh but fair. They were honest, with no hidden secrets lurking, and even though Alec had only met them once before, he liked them.

There were three elders—each of them with specific talents—Feliks, Yevgeny, and Asya. And they each in turn greeted Alec with a strong handshake and a warm smile.

Feliks was blond with a broad creased forehead. He was about forty in human years, stood under six foot tall, but had broad shoulders. Alec could imagine him as a lumberjack, and given his vampire talent was incredible strength, it didn't surprise Alec at all.

Yevgeny had fine brown hair that swept down into his eyes. He wore a peacoat and scarf, crossing the line between distinguished businessman and Bohemian poet. Younger in human years, he was the oldest of the three in vampire years at over two hundred and fifty. He was a pyro, though only through touch.

And finally Asya. She had a hard, angled face and her long black hair did little to soften her features. Despite looking nothing alike, she reminded Alec a lot of Jodis. Always the voice of reason, and quite possibly the glue that kept the coven together. Her talent was an empathic trait, in that she could sense if people were lying or not. In her role as elder in Russia, it was a talent that had served her and her coven well.

A brief round of reintroductions was had, but not entirely necessary. Though they never said so out loud, they were surprised to see Jorge and Adelmo in their company. "Thank you for allowing us to visit," Alec said. "You have seen the creatures?"

Feliks gave a hard nod. His English was brusque and broken. "Not directly. But words from others say yes. You think it be lycan creatures?"

"Yes," Alec admitted bluntly. "Unfortunately, yes. That's why we are here. I want to try and stop it before it begins."

"And you think it involves the Trinity Cathedral?"

Alec nodded. He knew the colorful Moscow church had been called a few different names throughout the years. "Yes. The design, the floorplan is an exact replica of the Göbekli Tepe pits, which was a portal for the Zoan. If you're willing, I can show you in your minds what we found."

The three Russian vampires nodded, so Alec showed them the aerial image of the Göbekli Tepe pits that Jodis and Viviana had showed them earlier. "This is the portal the Zoan came through." Then he superimposed the floor design of St Basil's cathedral over it making the two images merge perfectly.

Asya whispered. "Nine circles."

"It's like a replica," Yevgeny hissed. "The cathedral is another portal."

Alec nodded. "So it would seem. The circles represent the nine planets aligning in that particular formation for the corresponding circular design for the portal to open."

Asya's brows furrowed. "When?"

"Now," Jodis answered. "The sighting of a Zoan creature here cannot be a coincidence."

Yevgeny narrowed his eyes. "I'd hoped you were wrong, Alec. But I have called for Stas to come. He's no doubt arguing with the leaper who was sent to bring him back, but he will be here." Then he added, "But if you have the ability to leap him here without his say so...."

"I do," Alec allowed. "Though I'd prefer not to take away his free will."

Yevgeny smiled, and Alec could see this pleased the Russian elder. "Good, good."

"Who is Stas?" Cronin asked.

"Stas is a vampire, even older than us," Asya explained. "He was here in Moscow when the cathedral was built. He is a recluse of sorts, tends to go off-grid."

"How is that possible?" Eiji asked. "Forgive me for asking, but if he is older than you, why is he not considered an elder?"

Feliks sighed. "He refused. He decline to be leader."

Asya furthered, more kindly. "Stas can read minds. He prefers the life of solitude."

"Ah." Cronin, Jacques, Eiji, and Jodis nodded in understanding.

Alec smiled at Kennard, who hadn't said a word since they'd arrived. "What?" Kennard asked with his usual snark.

"Nothing," Alec said, biting his lip. "Nothing at all." He

didn't want to give anything away. But he turned back to the three Russian elders. "St. Basil's," he started. "I'm assuming there are crypts not known to the public and this is where the creatures were seen?"

Yevgeny smiled. "Of course. Crypts and tunnels between the cathedral and the Kremlin. Shall we go now? Or wait for Stas to arrive?"

Alec looked at the others, taking in their answers from their minds. He turned back to Yevgeny and shrugged. Unfortunately daylight would soon be upon them. There wasn't any time to waste. "Now."

THE INTERIOR ARCHITECTURE and design of St. Basil's cathedral was, for the want of a better word, incredible. "Wow," Alec whispered, taking in the room they'd leapt to. It was the central church within the cathedral. He took in every detail his perfect vampire sight allowed. The craftsmanship, the brickwork, and attention to detail was staggering.

Feliks smiled fondly as he looked over the high vaulted ceilings, tiled and painted walls, and the woodwork. "They do a good job, yes?"

"Promise me a tour when we have more time," Alec said. "I'd love to come back here one day and have a proper look, if that's okay?"

Asya gave a nod. "Of course. Any time."

Everyone took a moment to look up at the circular, pinnacled ceiling and the religious artwork that adorned the walls. Kennard let out a low breath. "Why are all paintings of religious persuasions so foreboding?" he asked. "It's...

creepy. The way they hold those crosses looks like they're about to stake us."

Alec stood beside him, taking in the dozens of paintings of priests, saints, and those of Mary and Jesus. "Not us," he said to the Russian vampires. "Zoan. I saw it in Gautier's mind. When Cronin asked how we kill them, I saw in his memory how he staked one in the chest with a cross."

The three Russian vampires stared at Alec, then back at a painting of baby Jesus holding a cross. Kennard scoffed. "Told you they were creepy."

Cronin frowned, his brow creased with worry. "There are no gargoyles on the outside of this building."

"Hmm." That was something Alec hadn't even given thought to. He looked at Viviana. "When was the last time the planets aligned to mimic the design of this cathedral?"

"1812."

"When Napoleon burned it down," Eiji said, his jaw clenched. "That can't be a coincidence."

Kennard hissed. His scathing opinion of Napoleon was no secret. "Nothing Napoleon did was a coincidence."

"He was trying to stop the portal?" Asya asked.

Alec shrugged and nodded at the same time. "It's possible. It's likely, even. Maybe he realized what a mistake Paris had been, or maybe he wanted to resume complete control. I don't know."

"Come. Priests will be here if we don't hurry," Feliks' voice boomed in the quiet. The huge Russian led them through the intricately bricked halls and stopped at an old wooden door. He opened it and had to bend to fit through it. "This way."

They went through more domed brick halls not open to the public, and Feliks waved his hand at the door of one locked room. Easily crushing the padlock between his two fingers, he opened the door and going inside, pulled up a wooden trapdoor in the floor. Grateful he didn't suffer claustrophobia, they proceeded down the narrow stone steps, which opened out to a vaulted-ceiling crypt. The archways were low, intricate tiles made art of the walls, and given there were now twelve vampires down there, there wasn't exactly a great deal of space. It was completely empty and before Alec could question him, Feliks led them to a crevice hidden in the corner.

"These are not known to the humans," Feliks said. "This tunnel goes to the church behind Kremlin walls."

Alec closed his eyes, and with a deep breath, he expanded his mind to gauge the space around him. "There is another level beneath us," he said.

The Russian vampires shook their heads, confused. "No," Yevgeny said. Alec could see in their minds that they truly believed this. They weren't being deliberately deceptive. They honestly didn't know.

"Yes," Alec said. "Like there was under the church in London. A hidden crypt."

Eiji took out his two wooden crosses from his thigh quiver. "I won't get caught off guard this time," he said.

Jodis took out two for herself as well, and Kennard held his hand out, taking the cross that Jodis offered him. "Me either. Creepy bastards," Kennard said. Eiji laughed and handed one to Benito as well.

"I can't sense anything," Alec explained. He held out his hand and pictured the smaller wooden crosses he saw in the center church above and leapt four of them into his hands.

The Russians startled at seeing the objects magically appear before them. Alec handed one to Cronin, then handed one each to Yevgeny, Feliks, and Asya. "Just in case."

"Just in case what?" Asya questioned.

"Just in case any Zoan are waiting for us, stab them with the cross," Alec said. The three of them nodded stoically. "And be careful," Alec added. "They can breathe fire."

Feliks swallowed hard and spat the words, "Eto piz'dets."

Alec smiled. The Russian wasn't far wrong. It *was* fucked up. He took a final look at the faces of those with him, each vampire armed and ready, alert and a little afraid. And lastly, he looked at Cronin. *My heart is yours, always.*

His reply was short and fervent. *As mine is yours.*

And with a deep breath and a silent prayer to whatever God was listening, Alec leapt.

CHAPTER FOURTEEN

FLAMES CAME at them from the closest Zoan creature as it roared hell and heat. Almost six feet of winged wolf, sharp teeth and claws, it screeched and thundered, and the sulfur-stench was rank.

The army of vampires scattered on reflex and the flames hit nothing but the dirt wall behind them.

The room was cavernous, huge and deep, and the nine circular pits were laid out just as the cathedral above it. The walls, floor, and ceiling were dirt, and the center pit was lined with nine pillars of stone. But that wasn't the most horrific thing. Because the center pit was also spewing out Zoan creatures, one after the other. Like they bubbled up from Hell, reborn and overflowing into the pit. Some were wolf-looking, some looked more reptilian. Some had wings, some had tails. They snapped and bellowed, screeched and howled.

Cronin had never seen anything like it.

Alec kept Jorge and Adelmo behind him and threw out his hands as he yelled, "Stop!"

But time didn't stop.

The creatures kept coming.

Eiji staked one with a cross and it screamed before turning into dust. Another set upon him, its belly and throat burning orange as if it were about to roar flames at him, and Jodis flew at it. She tried to freeze the creature's chest with her ability to turn things to ice, to extinguish its fire. It screamed at her, unharmed. She held a cross in each hand like a sword, and with such grace and beauty, she spun like a ballerina. Her hair twirled around her face like ribbons, and she stabbed the creature in the heart.

Kennard held his own, as did Benito and Viviana. The creatures seemed drawn to the furthest tunnel, the one Cronin assumed that led to the Kremlin, and some turned to attack the vampires.

Cronin kept close to Alec, to help defend Jorge and Adelmo, but also to be as close to Alec as he could. He knew Alec's powers and abilities outnumbered his a thousand to one, yet it would kill him to be anywhere else.

Alec used an array of weapons at the creatures: fire, ice, he stunned them, he tried to make them explode. Nothing worked.

"They're controlling time here," Alec said. "My powers are useless against them." Then he waved his hand, sending up a shield over the vampires. Cronin hoped it would at least deflect flames if a Zoan got close enough to fire upon them.

But the Zoan kept coming. The pit kept spewing out new creatures, each one more hideous and grotesque than the last. "We must shut down the portal," Yevgeny said as he took out a Zoan. "The pillars in the middle pit. Can we knock them down?"

Without waiting for an answer, Feliks jumped at the Zoan's very doorway and using a strength Cronin didn't think was possible, he pushed over one of the pillars. He smashed his cross into one Zoan and quickly jumped out of the pit. But they never stopped coming. They just kept crawling out of a nonexistent hole.

And then it happened.

Jodis had turned to protect Eiji, as she often did, and a Zoan creature came at her. It swiped its huge claws at her, and she recoiled just in time. The razor-like talons missed her by millimeters. Seeing she was off-balance, the Zoan used its huge weight to slam into her.

"NO!" Eiji cried, flying through the air at the same time Kennard did, and both vampires staked the creature together, turning it to dust. Jodis was on the ground, and for a moment Cronin's world stopped. Jodis was his dearest friend, his maker. He'd never known this life without her....

"Jodis!" Cronin and Alec yelled together.

After the longest second, finally she coughed. Zoan dust plumed out from her mouth, and Eiji pulled her up to her feet. "I'm okay," she said softly, weakly.

Eiji looked as wild as Cronin had ever seen him. "Alec! There are too many," Eiji yelled. "And that was far too close."

"I agree," Alec said. "Everyone gather in. I'm gonna try something else."

Everyone did as Alec asked, forming a kind of circle around Jorge and Adelmo. "We're a smaller target here!" Asya said, not liking the huddled formation.

Alec put his hands down and closed his eyes. Cronin stood in front of him, putting himself between Alec and the Zoan, and the creatures circled in on them.

Then with a rush of air from Alec, exact replicas of themselves, eleven cloned vampire doubles—Jorge wasn't replicated—appeared to their right. Then another eleven to their left. And another eleven across the pits, each armed and ready to fight. They started attacking the Zoan creatures, sending mass confusion amongst the creatures.

Alec swayed and fell backwards, and Benito caught him easily. "Alec!"

Cronin was quick to take him, holding him up, cradling him in his arms. "He's too weak from replicating. It exhausts him!"

Alec's eyes took a moment to focus on Cronin. "Get us out. But stay close. I need to be close to keep the replicas going."

"Everyone hold on," Cronin ordered. Adelmo picked up Jorge in his arms, and as soon as the twelve of them were touching, Cronin leapt them the hell out of there.

THE MAIN CHURCH of St. Basil's cathedral was a welcome reprieve to the buried hole directly below them that they'd just come from. Cronin knelt down and gently placed Alec on the tiled floor, resting his head and back on Cronin's lap.

"What's wrong with him?" Kennard asked. Concern etched his fine features.

"Replicating drains him," Cronin said. "And replicating that many people...."

"I'm okay," Alec said softly.

"You were tired before we came here," Cronin said, putting his hand to Alec's face. "You haven't fed in too long."

"I'm fine," he said again.

"You don't look fine, Alec," Kennard said.

Alec sat up a little. "I'm feeling better. When those

replicates expire, I'll be as good as new. I think," he added. "I've never done this many people before."

"How do we know what's going on down there?" Asya asked.

"I can see them," Alec told her. "I can show you all if you like."

"Alec, you should rest," Cronin said sternly. "Don't expend energy unnecessarily."

"We need to see what's going on," Alec reasoned. He closed his eyes and a second later an image played through Cronin's mind. More like a film than a memory, a vivid play-by-play of what was happening beneath their very feet.

The replicated vampires fought well. Three Eiji's, three Jodis', three Cronin's, three of everybody, all fought as though they were real. The Zoan certainly couldn't tell the difference, and many of them were speared through the chest.

"Look at me go," Eiji said. "I am good at this."

"I don't look half bad either," Kennard added. "Oh, good shot, Benito!"

Benito chuckled. "I've been practicing. Can't you tell?"

"It is like watching a video game," Yevgeny said. "Can I control what one of me does?"

Alec let out a shaky breath. "No. Your replicated selves would behave as you would. At least I think.... I've never done this before. Surprised it works, to be honest."

Even the replicated Cronin's never left Alec's side, concerned that he was too fragmented, spread too thin, to be his competent self.

"I'm okay," Alec whispered, just for Cronin. "I can feel your worry."

"Apologies," Cronin murmured. "I don't wish to impede you further."

Just then a wolf-like Zoan with claws and teeth like razors reared on its hind legs and lunged at a replicated Alec. A huge paw came down hard, piercing his chest, his heart, and Cronin could only watch as his world stopped turning, and Alec fell to dust.

An anguished roar ripped through the silence from the three replicated Cronin's in his mind. The real Cronin fell backwards onto his ass on the church floor. "Alec!"

Alec struggled to get up, scrambling weakly to console him. "I'm okay. It was just a replicated me. I'm here."

Cronin felt a wave of numbing relief roll through him, and he knew it came from Alec. He put the heel of his hand to his chest where the residual ache still lingered, and he shook his head. "Even still, m'cridhe. To see you die...." He shuddered. "I cannot bear it."

Alec sagged from exertion, and Cronin quickly pulled him against his chest. They sat on the floor, leaning against the wall while the others looked on, both at the two men on the ground and at the visions in their minds.

Benito let out a wail as a replicated Viviana turned to dust, and he quickly pulled his sister into his arms. Then a replicated Kennard was caught off guard and a winged dragon-like Zoan let an unholy fire wash over him. The real Kennard paled, and Jodis put her hand on his arm. "It's not real," she said softly.

Eiji knelt beside Cronin and put his hand on Alec. "We're losing down there."

"We need more of us," Alec said. His eyes pinched shut, he let out a heaving breath, and more replications appeared down in the fiery pits before he sagged in Cronin's arms.

"Alec no," Cronin sobbed. "Please stop."

He opened his eyes wearily. "I've fought worse." Then Alec paused, the way he often did when he was seeing something, a vision only he could see. "Where's Kennard?" he asked.

Kennard? What on earth for...? "He's uh, he's just here," Cronin said.

Alec smiled just as Kennard crouched down beside him. "I'm glad you're here," Alec said.

Kennard glanced at Cronin, then back to Alec. "What for?"

"To see this." Alec sat up a little, still leaning against Cronin's chest. "We have visitors arriving in three, two, one."

Right on cue, two vampires leapt into the main cathedral, vampires Cronin had never seen before. They did not exactly like finding themselves amongst a dozen strange vampires.

Yevgeny and Asya stepped forward. "It's fine," Asya said in Russian with her hands out. "You're safe here. Thank you for coming, Stas."

Stas was a huge man, even bigger than Feliks. He looked around the cathedral and recognized the place immediately. "What is this? Why you bring me here?" he barked in broken English.

"We need your help," Yevgeny said. "You know the history of this church and the lands on which it was built."

Alec's hand tightened on Cronin's arm, and smiling despite being exhausted, he gave a nod toward Kennard. The elf-like English vampire stood up slowly. His mouth dropped open and his hands fell to his sides, seemingly unable to take his eyes off Stas, a vampire who was almost double his size. "Wow," Alec mumbled.

Stas stared at Kennard for the longest moment, and he took a step back. "What sorcery is this?"

Then Kennard took a step forward. "You are him."

Stas shook his head, though his expression was one of wonder. "And you...."

Kennard nodded and took another step forward. Then he stopped and turned back to Alec. "He is Russian?"

Alec smiled and he leaned back, relaxing into Cronin's chest. Then Cronin felt it: the bloom of fate. The exact feeling he had when he saw Alec the very first time. He knew Alec was feeling the bond between Kennard and Stas, and Alec was sharing it with Cronin. His empathic ability absorbed the emotions of those around him, but this was something special.

Cronin kissed the side of Alec's head, and for the briefest moment in a world of madness, to witness something wonderful was humbling and magical. It was clear to see from the faces of those in the room that it reminded them of what they were fighting for.

"You." Stas pointed his huge finger at Kennard and he backed away. "Stay away from me."

Oh. Okay, so maybe not.

Alec put his hand up. "Stas."

The huge Russian vampire's eyes widened with shock and he turned to look at everyone. "What happened? My mind! What is this?"

"It was me!" Alec said. His voice croaked as he spoke. "My name is Alec. I have put a shield around your mind to block out the voices. It is temporary. It's just to give you some peace from the thoughts of others while you process what is happening."

Stas sagged a little, and he calmed down considerably. Cronin didn't know if that was Alec's doing or not or relief from having the voices in his head finally silenced, but either way, it worked.

Kennard looked torn between staying away like Stas

had asked and going to him. He put his hand to his chest. "My name is Kennard. I am an elder from London."

Stas tried to look away from Kennard, but it seemed he couldn't. He shook his head and put his hand out, as though signaling that Kennard should not come any closer. He looked back at Yevgeny. "Why have I been called here?"

"This church was built on sacred ground, yes?" Yevgeny said. "Over nine pits with stone pillars?"

Stas paled and took a small step back, which was answer enough that he knew of the pits.

"The portal is open," Feliks told him. "The creatures are spilling out of it."

Stas shook his head vehemently. "The portal must be closed."

"How?" Eiji asked.

Stas looked around the room. "I don't know. Ivan the Terrible built this church. You heard of Oprichnina and the Massacre of Novgorod? Well it was not state policy or a famine or plague. It was those hellish creatures that killed sixty-thousand of my people."

"Oh, Jesus," Alec whispered under his breath.

"Ivan built this place to stop the Zoan? Or to protect them?" Asya asked.

Stas glared hard at her. "What do you think? He was promised great power, but it sent him mad."

Alec put his hand to his forehead. "So this portal was open before?"

Stas gave one hard nod. "Yes."

"How was it closed?"

Stas shrugged. "It just stopped. Like I said, I don't know. The creatures just stopped coming."

Alec sighed. "Well, these aren't stopping." He flashed a brief image of the battle in the pits below into Stas' mind so he could see what everyone else saw. There weren't many replicates left, and those creatures just kept coming out of the ground. They were escaping through a tunnel and heading toward the Kremlin.

Stas' eyes were saucers. "How do you do these mind tricks? You have more than one talent? How is this so?"

"He is the key," Cronin said.

Stas looked at him disbelievingly, before the huge man smiled and bowed his head. "Oh," he said softly. "Forgive me. It is an honor."

"It's going to be all over soon if we can't stop this," Alec said, then squeezed his eyes shut. Cronin saw, as he assumed everyone did, that two, three, four, and five more sets of replicates appeared in the pits below against too many Zoan. He slumped breathless and fell back against Cronin.

"Tell us what you know of this place," Jodis said to Stas. "Quickly."

"Many have tried to burn it down, to damage the pits. But nothing worked." He kept glancing at Kennard and could only drag his eyes off him for a second before looking at him again. "The Illyrians, the French. Napoleon himself tried."

Kennard hissed. "I always hated Napoleon."

Stas finally smiled at him. "Me too." Kennard's resulting grin was huge.

"Something had to have happened in 1812," Viviana said. She looked at Jodis. "I wish I had our laptop and notepads. We could try and figure this out."

Alec groaned and the computer and notepads Viviana and Jodis had been working on, including the book St. Peter wrote, appeared on the altar. "Ask and you shall receive," Alec whispered.

"Alec, you must stop," Cronin whispered, holding him tight. Replicating dozens of vampires was draining enough, but adding in the mental shield on Stas, shielding his own mind, mental projections into others, leaping... it was all too much. The visions in Cronin's mind of the battle beneath them started to diminish, flickering in and out. "Your talents are making you too weak," Cronin said. "You're trying to do too much." Finally the visions gave out altogether.

Yevgeny gasped. "The mental projections are gone. We can't see down there."

"He needs to feed," Eiji said to Cronin. Eiji was full of concern. Kneeling beside them, he put one hand on Alec's forehead, then on his chest. Then he pulled up his shirt-sleeve and put his wrist to Alec's mouth.

"No," Cronin said. "From me." He couldn't bear the thought of Alec tasting anyone else, as foolish—as selfish—as it seemed. He just couldn't. He pulled back his sleeve and put his wrist to Alec's mouth. "Alec, m'cridhe, drink from me."

Alec's eyes took a moment to focus. He opened his mouth, his fangs slowly came down like even that was an effort, and he bit down and started to drink. Cronin tipped Alec's head back against his chest to allow the blood to run down his throat. Alec had bitten and drank from Cronin countless times since he'd become a vampire, each time a carnal act. But this was *oh so* very different.

Alec needed him, and Cronin would do anything —*anything*—to make him right. He ignored the sting of being bitten and the dull ache that spread up his arm as Alec fed. He simply pressed his lips to the top of Alec's head and let the love he felt for him bloom warmth in his chest, hoping Alec would feel it.

A soft purr from Alec told him he could.

Alec eventually pulled his teeth back and licked the wound on Cronin's wrist, sealing it closed. He sagged again and closed his eyes, though he seemed to be breathing better. Eiji finally smiled and patted Alec's arm before he stood up and went back to Jodis.

"I can still see down there," Alec said. Then he whispered to the room, "We're losing this fight."

Then Jorge, who had stood hidden behind Adelmo all this time, walked to the middle of the room and rocked back on his heels. His eyes went black. "Alec?" It wasn't Jorge's voice that came from the child's mouth. It was Alec's mother. Jorge turned to look at where Cronin and Alec sat slumped against the wall, and the little boy frowned. "Oh, Alec." He walked over to them and put his chubby hand to Alec's cheek. "Let Jorge help."

"How?" Cronin asked.

"Take Jorge to the central pit," Alec's mother said. "And we will show you. We know now how you can beat them."

Alec stared at Jorge for a long while, and Cronin could tell they were having a silent, private conversation. Then Alec looked up at everyone watching on. "It's the only way."

"No!" Adelmo barked. "Into the pit with those creatures? He's just a boy!"

Jorge looked up at Adelmo and held out his hand to him. Adelmo took Jorge's hand and he smiled up at the only father he'd ever known. "Jorge help," he said. It was a voice Cronin didn't recognize.

Adelmo looked to Alec with panic in his eyes. "Can you not replicate him?"

It was Jorge who answered. "Must be Jorge."

Adelmo sagged. His face crumpled. "He's just a boy."

Alec struggled to get to his feet, so Cronin helped him.

"Those in the afterlife will help," Alec said. "And we all will go to keep him safe. We will defend his life with our own."

Despite the tears in his eyes, Adelmo nodded. He looked around at the other vampires in the room. Alec was unsteady on his feet so Cronin kept him close. "We have to do this now," Alec said. He looked around the room. "Jodis and Asya, stay here and figure out how Ivan closed the portal. The rest of us will go to kill as many Zoan as we can. And when we're down there, we *all* protect Jorge."

Jodis put her forehead to Eiji's. "Be safe, my love." Eiji responded with nothing but a soft kiss to her lips.

Alec fisted Cronin's shirt, trying to muster the strength to leap everyone, but he exhaled in a rush. He looked at Cronin with vulnerable eyes and shook his head. "I can't."

"Everyone hold on," Cronin said. He waited until everyone there was touching, and he leapt them all back into the nine circles of hell.

CHAPTER FIFTEEN

THE ZOAN CREATURES spun around when Cronin and a dozen vampires appeared. Some turned to fight. Some fled. The replicated versions of themselves had killed a great many, though their losses were great too. Only a few remained. The stench was worse: fire and brimstone, acrid and burning.

"Too many have escaped," Feliks said. "They must be in the basements of the Kremlin by now."

Cronin agreed. And once daylight spread over Moscow, the vampires would be useless to fight them. The Zoan would run free through the city, killing everyone they found.

Stas stood stunned at the sight before him. He shook his head in disbelief and whispered, "I cannot believe my eyes."

A slinking wolf saw the opportunity to attack him and rushed at Stas. Kennard flew at the creature with two hands on his cross and stabbed it in the chest. "Not him," Kennard hissed as he turned the creature into dust.

Eiji threw him a spare cross, which Kennard then

offered to Stas. He took it and rewarded Kennard with a smile.

"Into the pit," Jorge said. The circle of vampires that surrounded and protected him moved the boy closer to the center pit. As they jumped down into the hollowed out earth, another Zoan bubbled out of the center. It squawked and screeched, and Eiji caught it by surprise with a cross to the chest.

"Good idea, Eiji! We can kill them as they come through the portal," Benito said. "Catch them off guard."

"Too many have escaped already," Feliks repeated, this time directly to Yevgeny. "Our city must be under attack. There must be hundreds of them!"

Still holding Alec up, Cronin looked around the large underground arena. The replicated vampires had taken out the last few Zoans that stayed to fight. Only one replicated Eiji and Cronin remained. Cronin looked at Feliks. "You and Yevgeny should go. Take the two replicates with you. And you." Cronin looked at the leaper who returned Stas to the cathedral. "Leap them to the Kremlin. Kill what you can." Then Cronin turned to Stas. "The choice is yours, my friend. Go with your compatriots or stay with us."

Stas looked directly at Kennard. "I stay."

Kennard grinned and Alec took in a deep breath. Cronin guessed he could feel the bond between Stas and Kennard fortify. He stood on his own two feet now, though he still leaned against him. "Alec?" Cronin questioned.

"I feel better," he said. "The replicated vampires are gone, save two. The power drain on me has lessened."

But another creature came through the earth, this one with wings and horns. Cronin had seen gargoyles like this on a building in Spain once.

Feliks roared back at the creature and killed it before it could even get its tail through the portal. "We go to Kremlin!" Feliks barked. With a nod from Yevgeny, the leaper put out his hand and along with the two replicates, they were gone.

It left Eiji, Benito, Kennard, and Stas with an unarmed Adelmo, a defenseless Jorge, a too-weak-to-fight Alec, and Cronin, who could not fight because he was holding up Alec. Not exactly the best team to take into battle, but it would have to do.

Just then there was an almighty series of screeching and bellows from down the tunnel where the creatures had run. "We don't have much time, they're coming back this way," Eiji said.

Then Jorge's head fell back. His eyes were a solid black. He rose up off the ground so his toes barely touched and he floated with his arms outstretched. A white light radiated from his black eyes and his open mouth, splitting the cavernous pits into blinding light.

Then like the gates of heaven opened against the pits of hell, vampires appeared. Apparitions, ethereal, unimaginable, and beautiful. The vampires once lost, returned.

Alec's mother was at the forefront, smiling serenely. Behind her stood Willem and Johan, side-by-side. And Mikka, the vampire who died in the alley the night Cronin finally found Alec. And behind them, scores of ghostly vampires. Dozens, if not hundreds of them.

"We've come to help. It was Willem who discovered how to beat them," Heather MacAidan said with a smiling glance to the man behind her. Then she put her hand to Alec's cheek. "These creatures spawn from the depths of evil, so only the good can stop them."

"They've escaped to the city," Alec said, nodding

toward the tunnel that ran to the Kremlin. "We can't stop them."

"*We* can stop them," she said. Her voice wisped in the air like bells. "You need to close the portal, Alec. Once and for all. As the key, it is your last and final quest."

Alec shook his head. "I don't know how to close it."

Heather smiled. "You'll figure out a way. You always do."

Then Willem walked to Cronin. He looked just as Cronin remembered, only now he looked... peaceful. Truly soul-enlightened, and happy. "Cronin, my old friend."

"Willem." Cronin nodded with a smile at Johan. "A match made in heaven, I see."

Willem laughed, a musical sound. "And yours is the key. There could only be one man good enough for you."

Alec bowed his head to Willem. "Thank you for coming, for helping us. I was rude to you before and I'm sorry. You're saving us and I am forever in your debt."

"Keep my friend here safe and I shall deem us even," Willem said with a smile. He turned to Cronin. "I always knew we'd meet on the battlefield once more, my dear Scotsman." Then he bowed his head. "Until we meet again."

They turned to go but before they were gone, Alec said, "Johan! Be careful down there."

Johan laughed. "They cannot harm what is already dead." As if to prove a point, a Zoan slithered from the portal. Mikka grabbed it and sunk his teeth into its neck. The creature screamed before it turned to dust.

Mikka dusted off his hands and gave a nod to Willem. "It works."

"Mikka," Cronin said. "I owe you eternal gratitude for saving Alec that night."

"It was my honor," he replied with a humble smile. Then all the ghosts turned their heads to a sound Cronin couldn't even hear.

Johan gave Cronin a smile and slid his hand into Willem's before they glided away down the tunnel with their army of ghosts behind them. Just a moment later, Zoan screams were heard down the tunnel.

Everyone turned to the sound, their attention drawn to the horrific howls of slaughter and mayhem that echoed back to them. And in that one split second, that one tiny moment, they were caught off guard.

"No!" Adelmo's voice rang clear.

Cronin turned just in time to see a small half-wolf, half-dragon creature rush at Jorge and Adelmo as he crashed into the beast. The Zoan's throat glowed orange and fire burst from its mouth. Flames engulfed Adelmo, stunning him, and in that split second, the creature speared Adelmo's chest.

And before anyone could move, Adelmo was gone.

As if in slow motion, Jorge blinked, then he crumpled with a wail, a scream of agony ripping from his lungs. Alec, with his empathic ability, stumbled backwards. He had his hand to his heart and he gasped for air. Cronin caught him, just as Heather picked up Jorge.

"Take the boy," she said. "You must go."

Alec couldn't stand fully upright. His breaths were ragged, his hands were shaking, feeling everything that Jorge felt.

Jorge finally sucked back a grated breath and sobbed. "Papa!"

"Take him," Heather repeated. She passed Jorge into Alec's arms and the little boy fisted his shirt and thrashed in his hold. "Close the portal. We'll take care of the rest."

Cronin hesitated. He didn't know where to go, where to leap them to.

Another creature slid out of the portal and Heather looked over her shoulder at Cronin. "Go!"

Eiji rounded up Kennard and Stas and pushed Benito toward Cronin so they were all touching. "To Jodis and Asya."

Cronin pulled Alec and Jorge against him, held out his free hand, and left Alec's mother to kill the beast.

JODIS AND ASYA both recoiled from their sudden appearance, stepping back at first but then crouching in a defensive position.

Until they saw who it was.

And how Alec was cradling Jorge.

"Adelmo?" Jodis asked. Eiji shook his head, and Jodis put her hand to her mouth. Then she studied Alec, how he could barely stand, how he held onto the boy, and her look of sorrow became concern. "And Alec?"

"He feels what Jorge feels," Cronin said. "We need to close the portal. Now. There's no saying how long Jorge's connection to the afterlife will last."

"My papa, my papa," Jorge sobbed over and over until his voice faded away to nothing. He lay still, his eyes open, his mouth still repeating the words *my papa* without the sound.

Alec went to his knees, still cradling the boy. "Oh, God," he rasped out. "The pain...."

Cronin kneeled before Alec and cupped his face. "Alec, you must compartmentalize the pain. You've done it before. Can you close it off?"

Alec shook his head. "It's too much. Their bond, it's broken!" He groaned through a ragged breath. "Jesus."

"Just try for me, m'cridhe," Cronin begged. Being Alec's mate, he could feel a fraction of what Alec could feel, and it truly was a bewildering pain. "Please."

Alec closed his eyes and took in a few deep breaths. Eventually he nodded. "I'm trying to shield it from you. I'm sorry, but that's the best I can do. It's so strong, Cronin. His heart, his soul... he's broken."

Cronin's eyes welled with tears. He could not even imagine the pain Jorge was feeling right now. The thought alone of losing Alec was crippling. Alec took another deep breath and exhaled slowly, but he clung to the child and slowly, slowly got to his feet.

It was then Cronin noticed everyone was standing, watching, and Jodis was crying. Eiji had his arm around her, Benito stood by his sister Viviana, and Stas was standing protectively at Kennard's side. There was an unwritten law amongst vampires that no one should ever lose their mate. It was Alec who had told them once that Adelmo and Jorge were fated. Not as lovers of course, but as father and son. It had been wondered for a century why the man would take on a perpetual child, especially one with such a misunderstood talent.

Fate. That's why.

No one questioned Jorge's sorrow. No one possibly could. The boy was, as Alec had said, broken. He lay in Alec's arms catatonic and lifeless. Utterly destroyed.

Alec held him tighter.

"Feliks? Yevgeny?" Asya asked, she looked so worried. "They live?"

Eiji nodded. "Yes. They're fine. They went to the

Kremlin to kill the Zoans that escaped, with the help of Willem and Johan's army."

Cronin tried not to sound impatient. "The portal?"

Asya held out a notepad. "We think we know where the gate is." She showed the picture she'd drawn. There were nine points in a circular formation with a middle point, like the spokes of a wheel. "When Alec was changed in Scotland, it opened the portal in Turkey. The planets aligned to mimic the Göbekli Tepe and in a different location, the Callanish Stones, you became vampire."

"So the gate we need to close is not here?" Eiji asked.

"I've seen that before," Alec said, looking at the picture. "Jorge told us in the beginning you know, he said it! *Stone circle, stone prison.* A circular design made from solid stone, and the missing gargoyles.... Jesus, I should have seen this." Alec shook his head. "Pennsylvanian penitentiary."

Cronin said, "We need floor plans, history, anything you can tell us about that place."

Jodis turned the laptop around so they could all see the screen and answered. "It's a wagon-wheel design with nine spokes. It was designed by a man called John Haviland. He spent time in both Paris and Moscow," she said, pausing a moment to let that sink in. "According to legend, he was commissioned to build the prison one night after long talks of his travels with one Benjamin Franklin."

"*The* Benjamin Franklin?" Alec asked.

Asya nodded. "The one and the same."

Alec shook his head again. "So he goes to Paris and Moscow where there are portal pits under churches, then comes back and builds a circular building with stone pillars with the help of Benjamin Franklin?"

"Benjamin Franklin was a Grand Master in the Freemason's. Maybe he knew something," Kennard said.

"Remind me to pay Dan Brown a visit when all this is over," Alec mumbled. "Is there anything specific or peculiar about the location of the penitentiary?"

"It was once land owned by the Lenape people, relatively peaceful Native American people who had a kinship with the wolf," Asya said, reading notes off the notepad. "They also told stories to their children of the *Mishipeshu*. A creature that was a mix of wolf and dragon that would eat them if they weren't well behaved."

"A lycan." Alec stared at Jodis. "The prison was built on the sacred grounds of an Indian tribe that feared the *lycan*?"

No one spoke, just looked around at each other as realization sank in.

"Well," Eiji said, breaking the silence. He pulled a bigger cross off the wall. "Then the Eastern State Penitentiary it is."

AFTER LEAPING TO THE PENITENTIARY, the first thing Cronin noticed was the color of the sky out the window. It was breaking pinks and yellows on the horizon, faint, but dawn was coming. And he doubted Alec had the power left in him to stop time.

Alec. His love, his heart.

His duty as the key was wearing him down, weakening him. And Cronin swore to himself right then and there, after this—if they survived it—he would take Alec away to where there was nothing but peace and quiet.

Alec pulled Jorge tighter against him. "We're almost done, kiddo," he said softly.

Jodis stood in front of Alec with her arms out. "Give him to me. I'll protect him while you go."

Alec hesitated at first, but reluctantly handed the lifeless boy to Jodis. When she had him cradled in her arms, Alec put his hand to Jorge's face, and what he said directly into Jorge's mind, Cronin could only guess. But Jorge's eyes closed and a tear escaped the boy's eye, sliding solitarily down to his temple before Alec stepped back and took a shaky breath.

"You're feeling better?" Cronin asked him.

He ran his hands through his hair and scrubbed his face. "I am. Jorge's pain is still there, but I have a better handle on it now. And the replicates are gone, so I'm not so drained."

Everyone breathed a sigh of relief. "Okay," Eiji said, holding the cross like a weapon. "We need to do this now."

"How?" Kennard asked. He looked around the old abandoned room they were in. "If this portal needs to close, we're going to need power, or something. In the Callanish Stones we had all the elements, we had the sun and the moon, and we had you, Alec." He looked around again and shrugged. "Here we have nothing."

"No," Alec said. "We have Benjamin Franklin."

"We have what?" Eiji asked.

"Benjamin Franklin," Alec repeated. "And what did he use to bring lightning to the ground?"

Eiji answered. "A kite."

Alec said with a smile. "A kite with what tied to it?"

Jodis answered. "A key."

Alec grinned and pointed to his own chest. "A key."

Cronin couldn't stop the low growl that rumbled in his chest. "You wish to use yourself as a conductor of lightning?"

"I did it before," Alec answered. "When I was changed from a human to a vampire, light from the circle went through me, yes? I have mercury in my veins."

Cronin ignored his question. "No, no, no. It cannot be safe."

"I don't see an alternative," he replied. "It has to be the way."

"Alec, wait!" Cronin said. "Please."

ALEC RAN down the first corridor toward the center guard tower. "Come on, we're running out of time."

They followed him down a stone hallway lined with prison cells on either side. Paint peeled from the walls of the two-story space and it smelled of mold, rust, and abandonment. When they got to the center watch tower, Alec skidded to a stop. Everyone filed in behind him, oblivious to the storm brewing outside.

Waiting for them were the five cloaked Zoan leaders who had haunted Alec from the beginning and the two huge stone gargoyle guard dogs. The gargoyles growled and gnashed their teeth, but the Zoan leader laughed. His cloak slid back from his face, revealing his razor teeth, wolf muzzle, and scaly head. They hadn't bothered with their human skins.

Eiji drew two crosses from his thigh holsters. "You'll meet the same fate as your pack did in Russia."

The leader didn't seem fazed. "It was a ploy for distraction."

"He wanted me here," Alec said as lightning flashed across the sky.

"The key's blood will serve us well," the leader said. His long tongue lashed at his teeth. His small beady eyes slid with vertical eyelids. "You think you're here to close the gate?" It laughed. "No, it will open all the portals over the planet."

"You're wrong," Alec said.

"When we met last time," the leader said, "I called you my enemy. A weak, insignificant adversary. But then I scratched you and smelled your blood. You have mercury in your veins."

"So what?"

"Then you are not my enemy," the Zoan replied. "You will help us."

"Never," Alec replied and thunder boomed outside. He drew two crosses like swords and the gargoyle watchdogs growled. "I'll die before I help you."

"Your blood, hot or cold, will help me," the leader sneered. "You can die all you like."

"When I die," Alec replied coldly, "I will turn to dust." Alec turned the cross around and put the point of the long end to his heart. "Maybe I should end it all for you now."

The leader snarled and the two gargoyle guard dogs lunged at him. Stas wrestled with one, throwing it against the far wall. Cronin leapt to the other one, cross extended out, and pierced its chest when he appeared underneath it, rendering it to dust. The first gargoyle roared a deafening sound. The other cloaked Zoan flew into defense mode.

They lunged and swiped, gnashing teeth, and the leader's chest glowed orange, a sign it was about to blow fire.

"Look out!" Kennard said and pulled Stas out of the way. The burst of flame caught him instead, and he turned for one moment to look at Stas before the Zoan buried its paw in Kennard's chest, sending a wisp of dust that was once Kennard, swirling to the floor.

Stas bellowed, louder than the gargoyle had, and flew into a rage. He smashed one Zoan, missing the leader, but collected another Zoan and ripped its head off with his bare hands.

The remaining gargoyle lurched at him and Eiji dove at it, rolling gracefully through the air and slicing the gargoyles chest cavity open. It half howled before it fell to dust and rubble.

The leader of the Zoan lashed its claws out, each talon as long as a knife blade, and it caught Alec on the arm. Cronin pulled Alec away, but it was too late.

The Zoan leader sniffed the air. Then it took a deeper breath. It gnashed its ghastly teeth. "No!"

"No mercury," Alec said. Then he laughed, just as thunder and lightning cracked through the sky.

The Zoan leader roared and breathed an unholy fire upon the vampires. Flames filled the room, turning each of them, Alec, Cronin, Eiji, and Stas to ash and dust.

Then the Zoan leader looked up toward the sky.

THE CENTER TOWER WAS DECREPIT, quickly losing its battle with age and weather, and Alec climbed atop the apex of the roof.

"Hurry Alec," Cronin said, standing back. He looked down at the center room below them, to where the Zoan leader was looking up at him. "They know those vampires were replicas of us."

Thunder crashed above their heads. The very storm was on top of them and static charged the air. Cronin knew it was coming. He could feel it.

The Zoan below scampered to climb the walls but couldn't find purchase on the degraded plaster. "Get him!" the leader called.

"I don't think so," Eiji's voice called out from one of the corridors on the ground floor. "Stay down here and fight the real me. You're nothing but a time-jumping maggot."

Cronin probably would have laughed at Eiji's art of distraction if he wasn't worried they were all about to die.

Lightning ripped the sky open and a gale tore through the guardhouse, almost blowing Alec off the watchtower. Cronin hung onto the guardrail as the storm whipped around them. Alec righted himself, extended his arms out wide, and waited for Benjamin Franklin's theory to work.

The three remaining Zoan stopped. One turned to face Eiji, while the leader and another started to climb the walls.

"Alec!" Cronin yelled above the storm.

Alec screamed at the sky. "You want to hold a key to the lightning? Then come get me!"

And the lightning did.

Sparking through the sky, a bolt of pure light ripped from the clouds, down to the closest metal it could find.

Alec.

His back arched, and if he was screaming or it was the roar of the storm, Cronin couldn't tell.

But the lightning went through him like it did when he was changed in the middle of the Callanish Stones in Scotland. The light beamed down to the ground floor and flashed down the nine spokes of the building, where it joined at the ends, creating a circle of light.

The light spun and turned, creating a spinning wheel of energy, and the Zoan fought to hang on. They clung to the handrails, ripped claw marks in the walls as the power of the light tore them from the room. The three remaining Zoan were flung into the air, wrenched up and into the sky and disappeared into the clouds.

The beam of light was sucked back in like a vacuum,

taking sound with it as it retracted back in and up the center of the circle. It held Alec for a second before releasing him and vanishing into the sky above.

Alec fell through the roof toward the ground two stories below. Cronin leapt, scarcely catching Alec before he hit the ground. His eyes were closed, he wasn't moving. He was barely breathing.

"Alec?" Cronin whispered.

Eiji stepped into the circular room. "Is he...?"

Kennard and Stas followed Eiji in, both with worry on their faces. Benito and Asya soon followed. "Alec?" Kennard whispered.

Cronin put him gently on the floor. "Alec? Can you hear me?" An eternity passed. One second seemed a thousand years. Cronin fought tears and his voice wouldn't work at first. "Alec? Come back to me, m'cridhe."

Alec slowly opened his eyes, and after a faint heartbeat, he spoke. "Did we win?"

Cronin pulled Alec against him. "Oh, my heart. You scared me."

Eiji knelt down beside him. "You did good, Alec. But I think I'm done with excitement for a while, yeah?"

Alec sat up a little. "Me too."

But then Jodis walked in, holding a lifeless Jorge in her arms like a ragdoll. His black eyes, once shining with excitement, were now dull. Jodis had been crying, or perhaps, crying still. "Alec," she said softly. "I think he's dying."

Jorge's head lolled to the side. Jodis gently placed him in Alec's arms. Then Alec said, "We're about to have a visitor," just as Heather appeared. The ghostly apparition of Alec's mother smiled sadly at her son, then at the boy he cradled in his arms.

"Mom," Alec said. "Did the portal close?"

She nodded. "Yes, you did it."

Alec sighed in relief. "Oh, thank God."

Heather shook her head and smiled kindly. "No. Thank you, Alec. Thank all of you."

Jorge let out a sob, and Alec brushed the hair back from the little boy's forehead. Alec looked up at his mother. "He can't survive this, can he?"

Heather smiled sadly, then she knelt down in front of him and put her hand to Alec's face, then to Jorge's. "Jorge," she cooed, "there is someone here to see you."

Then like he walked out of thin air, Adelmo appeared. A flickering apparition, but Adelmo all the same. "Thank you for caring for him." His voice sounded like wind through the trees.

The sound of Adelmo's voice stirred something in Jorge and he roused from his listless state. He looked around the room, his eyes still all black, and he saw his father. He scampered out of Alec's arms. "Papa! Papa!" Jorge cried and ran to him. "Jorge stay with Papa! Jorge stay with Papa!"

"Oh," Alec started to say, no doubt wondering how on earth to break it to a perpetual six-year old that he would be without his Papa for eternity. He would be orphaned, forever. He'd never grow up, he'd never be old enough to understand that parents weren't around forever. Cronin recognized that losing a father was something Alec was struggling with himself.

"He can stay if he wants," Alec's mom said.

"He can?" Alec asked. "Because he can stay with me and Cronin if he wants. We'll look after him." Alec's mother smiled sadly, and Cronin squeezed Alec's hand.

"Papa," Jorge said. "Jorge stay with Papa."

Adelmo wiped the tears from the little boy's cheeks. "Is this what you want? What about Alec?"

"Alec is Jorge's friend," Jorge said, not taking his eyes off Adelmo.

"Will you stay with him?" Adelmo asked.

Jorge's little hands fisted Adelmo's shirt. "Jorge stay with Papa." Then Jorge looked at Heather. "Jorge can stay in the pretty place with his Papa?"

Heather smiled ethereally, and nodded.

Jorge smiled his little fanged smile and hugged his father's neck, and he started to cry again. "Jorge was sad. Jorge thought he lost his Papa."

Adelmo gave Alec a teary smile. "Thank you." Jorge turned in Adelmo's arms, and with a single wave of his chubby hand, they were gone.

Alec took a deep but shaky breath, and Cronin pulled him against him, kissing the side of his head. "Oh, m'cridhe."

Heather stood silent and waiting, and when Cronin released Alec, his mother took his hand. "Ailig, my beautiful boy," she said. "Can I ask you something?"

Alec nodded.

"If you wish to relinquish your powers, just say the word."

Alec was clearly surprised by this. "You can do that?"

Heather nodded. "Of course. And you've said a few times now you'd rather be without them."

"You heard me?" he said softly.

"We hear everything," she replied.

"Oh God," Alec cringed. "You see *everything...*?"

Heather laughed, a chiming of bells. "We don't look in bedrooms, Alec. Or on dining tables, or over sofas, or in the shower—"

Cronin cleared his throat, wanting the earth to swallow him whole.

Eiji laughed the loudest, and Heather raised an eyebrow at him. "Or on futons."

Eiji shut up after that.

Heather smiled fondly at Alec. "Just say the word."

It was silent between them for a moment, and Cronin had no doubt they were having a silent conversation. Then Heather cupped her hands to Alec's face and kissed his forehead. "Consider it done."

And she was gone.

Everyone stood in silence staring at Alec. *Had he really just given up every power known to vampires? Did he?*

Alec wiped his eyes with the back of his hand and looked up at the sky. The storm was gone as quickly as it came in, and the sun was starting to rise. "We need to leave," he said. He slid his arm around Cronin's waist and held on tight—the way he used to travel when Cronin leapt... before Alec had powers.

With not a word spoken, but questioning eyes from everyone, Cronin held out his hand. Everyone touched him, and they were gone.

EPILOGUE

IT HAD BEEN three months since the Zoan incident, and the New York apartment was blessedly quiet. Eiji and Jodis were enjoying some time alone in Japan. Kennard and Stas were in the Lithuanian forest—Alec couldn't believe Kennard agreed to go anywhere but London—Benito and Viviana were back in Italy, the Russian elders were safe in Moscow, Jacques had gone to Paris to help the new elders, and Kole and Eleanor had gone to the theater.

The world elders agreed that because the portal opened before they could hold their meeting, Alec wasn't to be held accountable for acting without counsel. Not that it mattered anyway—Alec had told them he was done. Though he was glad, out of all this mess, the one good thing to come from it was that there was now a governing body of twelve world elders. Cronin, Jodis, and Eiji were a part of it, and Alec of course—even though he wasn't an elder. But the pressure was off him alone now and dispersed onto the shoulders of wiser, more deserving vampires.

So while there had still been meetings, there had been a

lot more peace and quiet. Still not enough for Alec's liking though.

Cronin took Alec's hand, pulled him to his feet from where he sat on the sofa, and kissed him softly. "Close your eyes."

"I hate surprises," Alec whined as he closed his eyes. He didn't really. He loved surprises. But he just pretended he hated them.

"No you don't. You love them," Cronin said with a laugh. "Now keep them shut until I say so."

Alec felt them leaping but didn't want to ruin Cronin's happiness, so he closed his mind down and allowed himself to simply see nothing.

Alec knew they were in a small room somewhere. His vampire senses told him there were four walls surrounding him only a few feet away. But he felt no threat. In fact, he felt something else.

Cronin's breath was close, and Alec could tell he was smiling when he spoke. "Open your eyes."

They were standing in a room with white walls and dark wooden beams that held a low ceiling just above their heads. There was an empty fireplace and not much else. But Alec automatically knew where he was. The view out the window confirmed it, even though it was night outside. Alec could see across the field to the river. They were standing in the farmhouse at the field of Dunadd. The field where they would leap to for privacy. The field where a human Cronin had died, the small farmhouse Alec had once said he'd love to own.

He spun to look at Cronin. "How...?"

"Keeping secrets from you is not easy," Cronin said. "But keeping it a secret from the others was the hardest part." He smiled as he recalled Eiji's blatant inability to keep his mouth shut, let alone his mind.

Alec saw where Cronin's thoughts had taken him. "He knows," Alec said. "About my powers. He's just pretending he doesn't."

"Really?" Cronin's eyebrows rose to his hairline.

Alec chuckled. "Not at first. In the beginning he thought I'd relinquished my powers like everyone else did, but I'd catch him looking at me. His mind was curious, always looking, then one day he thought something funny and I laughed. He never said anything, but he smiled at me, and he knew."

"And he said nothing?"

Alec breathed in deeply, feeling more content than he had in a long time. "He knows I don't want the world to know. I'm happy with the vampire world thinking I'm powerless now. Well, except for the Elder Council. They know of course. But it allows us to be normal, for a while anyway. Until the next imminent threat. Though I don't think it will take Stas long to realize I've still shielded his mind... if Kennard lets him up for air long enough for him to even think of other things."

Cronin laughed at that. "I thought we were supposed to be rid of all duties of the key for a few hundred years," Cronin said. He kissed Alec with smiling lips.

It was true. From what Viviana and Jodis could determine, the next portal opening would be in two hundred and fifty-eight quiet years when the planets aligned with the design of the world-famous Hagia Sophia church in Istanbul. Nine circle design over the great Byzantine Cistern, which of course was built over nine open pits....

"Fingers crossed," Alec agreed. "Two hundred and fifty-eight years is a good start, but I have no doubt that someone will get too big for their boots and try for good old world domination. Not now, but in a hundred years, a thousand... I don't know." The truth was, when Alec was offered the very real option of relinquishing his powers, he'd said no. As much as his talents were a burden, he couldn't bear the thought of Cronin, or any of his friends, being in danger and not being able to save them. That, and the fact he'd not explored the talent of replicating as thoroughly as he'd liked. Cronin was rather fond of going to bed with two Alec's.

Cronin smiled. "So we have a little while to ourselves, yes?"

Alec nodded. "Peace and quiet, and fornication."

Cronin barked out a laugh. "It was normalcy you wanted."

Alec looked around the small, empty room. "And normalcy I got. I cannot believe you bought this place."

"I thought to furnish it and a little remodeling, but wanted your input. It is, after all, our new home."

Alec put his hand to his mouth. "You really bought it?"

Cronin nodded. "You mentioned wanting to purchase it, though you said it was only an errant thought. But after all we've been through, even if we have forever, I would say life is too short to be left wanting."

"Oh."

"I sold the apartment in London, which easily covered the cost of it," Cronin told him. "The land was the most expensive part. As you can see, the house is rather humble."

"The house is perfect."

And it was. Small. Private. Home.

Alec took Cronin's hand and pulled him into the next room. It was a sitting room, a small living area. "We can put the shelves of memorabilia along that wall," he said. Then moved into the next room, the master bedroom. "And this could be our room. The bed can go here and a shelf on that wall for your ax and helmet—"

"And Ra's sun disk and Emperor Qin's stone plate," Cronin added. He was smiling brilliantly.

"And we'll need to do the spare room for when Eiji and Jodis visit and my dad. And Sammy the cat will love it here," Alec went on, now walking into the bathroom. "Oh." He stopped, looking at the hideous tiles and ancient fittings. "Well, this will need redoing, because... well, yuck."

Cronin laughed. "We'll need to do a lot of remodeling, Alec. The windows need to be replaced with the UV filtered glass. I want the metal security plating that I installed in New York, though I'm not certain such an old building will handle such improvements—"

His words were cut off by Alec taking his face in both hands and kissing him soundly. He pulled back with a smile, then taking his hand again, he led him outside into the peaceful night. The view over their field, the blanket of long grass to the tree-lined river under the Scottish moon was perfect.

"This is ours?"

Cronin gave a nod. "Technically, it's yours."

Alec stared at him. "What?"

"I bought it for you."

Alec opened his mouth, then promptly snapped it shut. It was such an extravagant thing to do. Such a thoughtful, most perfect gift.

"It is for both of us," Cronin amended, clearly not sure of Alec's reaction. "It is our home. We will live here, if that is what you want."

Alec laughed and the sound rang out over the field. He'd never wanted anything more. "It's so perfect, Cronin!" He looked down toward the river. "You know, we could have a house warming party and make it a surprise wedding."

"A wedding? Are we not already wed?"

"We've done the hand-tying wedding, but not the wedding ring kind."

Cronin's eyes widened. "Alec, if you wished for a wedding ring you should have said-"

Alec cut him off with a laugh. "You'd think I'd be sick of anything to do with circles, but I would like to wear a metal band on my finger that says 'I belong to Cronin'." Before Cronin could answer, Alec showed him the vision from Cronin's human memory, of the wedding so long ago. The music played, and the newly wedded couple danced. The vision was faded, but the emotion was anything but. "We could dance," Alec whispered. "Like they danced. You longed for it back then, and now you shall have it."

Cronin's eyes closed and he started to purr, and. Alec could see in Cronin's mind how much he would love that, he could feel it in his heart. "M'cridhe."

Alec kissed him softly. "My heart."

Cronin reached into his pocket and held out his hand. On his palm was a single key. It was old, Alec guessed from the 1800s sometime. Cronin offered it to him. "It unlocks the front door. It is yours."

Alec slowly took the key and he smiled at the irony. A key for the key. Cronin's key. Then, closing his eyes, Alec replicated himself. The second Alec stood behind Cronin, and Alec chuckled as Cronin's purr became a growl. "You said you kept your talents to protect me," Cronin whispered breathily. "Yet I think your true reasons were for this." He let his head fall back onto the second Alec's shoulder and let the real Alec kiss down his neck.

Alec smiled as he kissed up Cronin's jaw, and the

second Alec ran his hands around Cronin's front to palm his dick. "You might be right." They led Cronin inside their new home and laid him on the floor, where each Alec wrung every ounce of pleasure from Cronin's body.

Afterwards, when the replicated Alec had served his purpose, and the real Alec and Cronin were sprawled out on the cottage floor, Alec sighed. There was nothing but peace and quiet, and a bone deep contentment. "Can we spend the next thousand years here?"

Cronin smiled at that. "And then some."

~The End~

CHARACTER/COVEN LIST

East Coast (New York) Coven:

Ailig "Alec" MacAidan
Cronin.
Eiji.
Jodis.
Eleanor.
Jacques.
Johan.
Mikka.

English (London) Coven:

Kennard.

Italian (Roman) Coven:

Benito.
Viviana.

Bolivian Coven:

Adelmo.
Jorge.

French (Parisian) Coven:

Corrina.
Gautier.

Russian (Muscovite) Coven:

Feliks.
Asya.
Stas.
Yevgeny

Egyptian (Fatmid and Mamluk) Covens:

Bes.
Keket.

Ancient Egyptian Coven:

Ammit.
Annubis.
Isis
Osiris.
Ra.

Illyrian Coven:

Riland (Autariatae coven)

Keket's guards.

Chinese Coven:

Emperor Qin.

Other Covens mentioned:

Yersinian (Black Plague)
West Coast Coven.
Pennsylvanian.
Mayan.
Spanish.
Atzec.
Buenos Aires.
Indian.

Humans:

Kole MacAidan
Heather MacAidan
Campbell.
Archbishop Gänsen.

Police:

De Angelo.
Cavill.
Patel.
Steinberg.

Dead Vampires:

Willem.
Heather MacAidan.
Johan.
Mikka.

ABOUT THE AUTHOR

N.R. Walker is an Australian author, who loves her genre of gay romance.
She loves writing and spends far too much time doing it, but wouldn't have it any other way.

She is many things: a mother, a wife, a sister, a writer. She has pretty, pretty boys who live in her head, who don't let her sleep at night unless she gives them life with words.

She likes it when they do dirty, dirty things... but likes it even more when they fall in love.

She used to think having people in her head talking to her was weird, until one day she happened across other writers who told her it was normal.

She's been writing ever since...

Email:
nrwalker@nrwalker.net

ALSO BY N.R. WALKER

Blind Faith (Blind Faith #1)

Through These Eyes (Blind Faith #2)

Blindside: Mark's Story (Blind Faith #3)

Ten in the Bin

Point of No Return – Turning Point #1

Breaking Point – Turning Point #2

Starting Point – Turning Point #3

Element of Retrofit – Thomas Elkin Series #1

Clarity of Lines – Thomas Elkin Series #2

Sense of Place – Thomas Elkin Series #3

Taxes and TARDIS

Three's Company

Red Dirt Heart

Red Dirt Heart 2

Red Dirt Heart 3

Red Dirt Heart 4

Red Dirt Christmas

Cronin's Key

Cronin's Key II

Cronin's Key III

Exchange of Hearts

The Spencer Cohen Series, Book One

The Spencer Cohen Series, Book Two

The Spencer Cohen Series, Book Three

The Spencer Cohen Series, Yanni's Story

Blood & Milk

The Weight Of It All

A Very Henry Christmas (The Weight of It All 1.5)

Perfect Catch

Switched

Imago

Imagines

Red Dirt Heart Imago

On Davis Row

Finders Keepers

Evolved

TITLES IN AUDIO:

Cronin's Key

Cronin's Key II

Cronin's Key III

Red Dirt Heart

Red Dirt Heart 2

Red Dirt Heart 3

Red Dirt Heart 4

The Weight Of It All

Switched

Point of No Return

Breaking Point

Spencer Cohen Book One

Spencer Cohen Book Two

FREE READS:

Sixty Five Hours

Learning to Feel

His Grandfather's Watch (And The Story of Billy and Hale)

The Twelfth of Never (Blind Faith 3.5)

Twelve Days of Christmas (Sixty Five Hours Christmas)

Best of Both Worlds

TRANSLATED TITLES:

Fiducia Cieca (Italian translation of Blind Faith)

Attraverso Questi Occhi (Italian translation of Through These Eyes)

Preso alla Sprovvista (Italian translation of Blindside)

Il giorno del Mai (Italian translation of Blind Faith 3.5)

Cuore di Terra Rossa (Italian translation of Red Dirt Heart)

Cuore di Terra Rossa 2 (Italian translation of Red Dirt Heart 2)

Cuore di Terra Rossa 3 (Italian translation of Red Dirt Heart 3)

Cuore di Terra Rossa 4 (Italian translation of Red Dirt Heart 4)

Confiance Aveugle (French translation of *Blind Faith*)

A travers ces yeux: Confiance Aveugle 2 (French translation of *Through These Eyes*)

Aveugle: Confiance Aveugle 3 (French translation of *Blindside*)

À Jamais (French translation of *Blind Faith 3.5*)

Cronin's Key (French translation)

Cronin's Key II (French translation)

Au Coeur de Sutton Station (French translation of *Red Dirt Heart*)

Partir ou rester (French translation of *Red Dirt Heart 2*)

Faire Face (French translation of *Red Dirt Heart 3*)

Trouver sa Place (French translation of *Red Dirt Heart 4*)

Rote Erde (German translation of *Red Dirt Heart*)

Rote Erde 2 (German translation of *Red Dirt Heart 2*)

Made in the USA
Monee, IL
07 July 2024

61311606R00142